# GUNSMOKE BONANZA

## Chuck Martin

**GUNSMOKE**

First published in the UK by Golden Lion

This hardback edition 2011
by AudioGO Ltd
by arrangement with
Golden West Literary Agency

ISBN 978 1 445 85629 2

**British Library Cataloguing in Publication Data available.**

Printed and bound in Great Britain by
CPI Antony Rowe, Chippenham and Eastbourne

# GUNSMOKE BONANZA

**Charles M. Martin** was born in Cincinnati, Ohio. In 1910 he worked for the California Land and Cattle Company. In 1915 he fought in Mexico as a mercenary soldier on the side of Pancho Villa. Later he worked on cattle ranches in various parts of the American West, sold paint products in Japan and China, was briefly a cowboy singer in vaudeville, and was a rodeo announcer in such places as Madison Square Garden in New York City and the Cow Palace in San Francisco. He began writing Western stories for pulp magazines in the early 1930s and continued to do so until the 1950s, something that in terms of his authentic background he was certainly capable of doing with a degree of verisimilitude. He published his first novel in 1936, *Left-Handed Law*, and followed it with *Law for Tombstone* (Greenberg, 1937). These novels introduced his character, Alamo Bowie, a Wells Fargo trouble-shooter and gunfighter. The character appealed to movie cowboy, Buck Jones, and both novels were made into motion pictures by Buck Jones Productions, *Left-handed Law* (Universal, 1937) and *Law for Tombstone* (Universal, 1937), with Buck Jones as Alamo Bowie. Martin was personally a brawling, hard-drinking individualist after the fashion of many of his fictional heroes. He carried on feuds with magazine and book editors as well as other writers. He worked so hard at his writing—at one time producing a million words a year for the magazine market—that on at least one occasion he suffered a nervous breakdown. In 1937 he began signing his name as Chuck Martin. He believed so passionately in the characters he was writing about that in the back yard of his home in southern California he created a graveyard for those who had died in his stories and by 1950 there were over 2,000 headstones in this private boothill. His stories always display great energy and continue to be read with pleasure for their adept pacing and colorful characters.

# CHAPTER ONE

A stuttering pair of shots blasted the twilight quiet of Three Points which stood at the entrance to Hell's Half Acre. Gospel Cummings raised his head to listen; then he arose from his chair in the tight little cabin he had built. As the caretaker of Boot Hill, he was handy to his work.

"Two fellers shooting, and one shot second," the bearded plainsman murmured knowingly. "It could have been a draw, but those Strip outlaws are fairly accurate with their hardware."

An old Bible was open on the deal table, and on the floor under the table stood a quart of Three Daisies whiskey. Gospel Cummings was a man with a dual personality; strong drink was his besetting sin, admittedly.

Now he stood in the open doorway, six feet and a bit. His age might have been anywhere from forty to fifty; the silky brown beard was deceptive. A black-butted six-shooter rode in a low-slung holster on his sturdy right leg; it was the right side where the bad man of his nature had its abode. The Book was always carried in the left tail of his long black coat.

Cummings put on his black Stetson and left the cabin. He walked slowly between the rocky pillars which marked the entrance to Hell's Half Acre, and his step was reverent.

The quiet of a dying sun hovered over the place of the dead. A horseman was disappearing over a ridge leading to the mesas toward the west. A faded gray Stetson rested on an unmarked headstone at the end of a long row. Cummings made his way unerringly to the discarded headgear.

The body of a man was lying beside the headstone; he was staring at the red sky with sightless eyes.

"Yeah, he shot—second," Cummings murmured in his beard. He leaned forward for a closer scrutiny. "Pete Lagruel He was *segundo* to Cord Demingway."

Gospel Cummings glanced at the discarded hat. Two gold pieces were lying on the brim, double his usual fee. Cummings took the twenty dollars and slipped the coins in a vest pocket.

"The way of the transgressor is hard," he murmured. "And the wages of sin is death. I'll notify Boot Hill Crandall, and John Saint John!"

Darkness had fallen when he rode up the wide dusty street of the little cattletown. A light showed from the office of the adobe jail, which meant that the deputy sheriff was at home. Cummings reined in at the rail and dismounted.

"Come in, Gospel," a deep voice invited. "The mesa outlaws are on the loose again, and I might need some help."

Cummings stepped into the office and nodded at an incredibly tall man who wore the badge of a deputy sheriff. John Saint John was six feet six, and weighed two hundred and forty pounds of hard bone and rawhide muscle.

"You eat yet?" he asked.

Gospel Cummings shook his head. "I'll eat after I make my report," he answered. "Pete Lagrue was killed back in Hell's Half Acre just about late sundown. I left him for the law and the coroner."

"That murdering owl-hooter had a killing coming long since," the deputy declared approvingly. "Who committed this law-abiding crime?"

"Couldn't say," Cummings replied. "He was *segundo* to the ramrod of that outlaw gang, Cord Demingway. It could have been some of Cord's work, because Pete was unusually fast with his tools."

"But Demingway was faster," Saint John answered. "Let's go up to Chinaman Charley's and put on the feed bag. This is on the law; you can ride back with me and point out the position of the corpse."

They left Cummings' horse at the rail, and walked up the street to a small lunchroom. These two had been friends for fifteen years, each independent in his own individual manner. Cummings had helped the law as many times as he had refused; when he had refused, it had been due to the deputy's domineering manners.

"We ain't had a planting in Boot Hill in a month," Saint John remarked, over the pie and coffee. "Did they pay your fee?"

"In advance," Cummings admitted reluctantly. "I'll get a few provisions before we ride back to Three Points."

"Fat Farrel up at the Casino says to tell you your credit is still good," Saint John remarked carelessly. "A man never knows when he might come down with a wracking cough."

"Or get bit by a snake," Cummings added grimly. "I'll pick up my merchandise and meet you at the jail. Like as not you will want to notify the coroner."

"Don't tell me how to do my law routine," the big man growled. "Your hands are shaking."

Gospel Cummings glared and rose to his feet. He left the lunch room, walked up to the Casino, entered the rear door, and coughed suggestively. He jerked when something touched his arm in the dark, but a smooth voice spoke quietly.

"Kill this one a customer paid for and left," the bartender suggested.

"I take that kindly, Fat," Cummings murmured

gratefully. "Wrap me up four quarts."

Fat Farrel came back with a package wrapped in newspaper. "Three dollars, at six bits a quart," he said quietly. "If you are short, I'll put it on the cuff."

"Take it out of this," Cummings answered, and gave Farrel a ten-dollar gold piece.

The bar-dog took the coin, tested it with his teeth, and asked a question. "Who got rubbed out?"

"Pete Lagrue; Saint John is riding back with me to bring in the body. Looks like either Pete or the gunnie who beat him to the shot picked out Pete's grave."

"I better tell Ace Fleming, the boss," Farrel commented. "He had some trouble on the Circle F with that outlaw gang; they've been rustling his beef for camp-meat. Not that Ace objects much to a man eating, but these cow-thieves kill a critter and just take the choice cuts. They leave the rest for the coyotes and other varmints."

"Take care of yourself, friend" the gaunt plainsman remarked, and he stepped into the alley and made his way to the jail.

He wondered about Ace Fleming who owned the Casino, and also the Circle F cattle ranch. Fleming was a square gambler, one of the smallest men in the district, and also one of the strongest. He stood five-feet-four in his high-heeled boots, was incredibly fast and accurate with a six-shooter, and did not know the meaning of fear. As Cummings rounded the alley corner, the gambler spoke softly from the shadows.

"Did you find Pete Lagrue?" he asked.

"Howdy, Ace; I found him in the graveyard."

"I killed him on Circle F range," Fleming said wonderingly.

"Thou shalt not kill, friend," Cummings admonished. "I saw a horsebacker riding away from Hell's Half Acre, and it wasn't you."

"I caught him killing a Circle F beef," Fleming explained. "There were two of them; one got away."

"So he piled the deceased on his horse and lugged him down to the burying ground," Cummings said. "Funny about that; I heard two shots, close together."

"That was just to bring you on the run," Fleming surmised. "What I wanted to say was this. I always bury my dead; here's a hundred dollars for Boot Hill Crandall, the undertaker. I'd rather not appear in the matter. You'll do this for me?"

"Count it done, Ace," Cummings agreed. "How is Sandra?"

"She gets lovelier every day," the little gambler answered quietly. "I'll always be in your debt for introducing us."

"I might have been her father," Cummings answered with a sigh. "But I could not control my appetite for strong drink."

"No man here has ever seen you under the influence," Fleming said loyally. "I wish my sins and shortcomings were as few as yours."

A black-covered wagon left the alley across the street, pulled by two black horses, with a tall thin man on the driver's seat. This would be Boot Hill Crandall, who operated the furniture store, and did the local undertaking as a sideline. He also chiseled appropriate epitaphs on the volcanic headstones for a dollar a letter. Cummings joined Saint John and spoke briefly.

"Making it easy on yourself, eh Saint? I saw Boot Hill driving toward Three Points."

"That's his business," the deputy answered grimly. "He gets forty dollars for a county case, and digs the grave."

Cummings mounted his horse with his package under his left arm. Saint John had saddled a big gray, and the two men left town and turned toward the west. They overtook and passed Crandall and his wagon, but they waited at the entrance to the graveyard until Crandall came along at a walk.

"I don't cater to these charity cases," Crandall complained. "Costs me three dollars to have the grave dug."

"Give him a good coffin," Cummings said slowly. Here's a hundred dollars a friend asked me to pass along to you."

"Who was this friend?" Saint John asked suspiciously.

"I promised to keep his identity in confidence," Cummings replied.

"You can't withhold evidence from the law!" the deputy bellowed. "I demand to know who paid for this burying!"

Gospel Cummings sighed. "You never learn, law-dog," he said patiently. "Now you just keep on demanding until Doomsday, and see what it buys you. Come on, Crandall." And he led the way to the dead man.

There was just enough light left for Crandall to tool his team between the headstones. Cummings helped him lift the dead outlaw to the wagon, and Saint John dismounted and came up to make his official examination.

"One of two gun-hawks did that killing," the deputy guessed shrewdly. "Cord Demingway or Ace Fleming could beat him to the shot." He stared at Cummings as Crandall drove out of the burying ground. "Which one was it?" he demanded.

"Ask them both," Cummings answered quietly. "You can always find Ace Fleming."

"Meaning I can't catch Demingway?" the deputy asked sharply.

"Up to now you haven't," Cummings reminded him. "That outlaw crowd has been back on the mesas going on two years. Well?"

"Well what?"

"What are you going to do about it?" Cummings asked.

"Let's get back to your cabin and sample that merchandise you bought," Saint John suggested.

They rode back to the cabin, and Cummings off-saddled and stabled his horse. Saint John tied up at the rack. He followed Cummings in and glanced at a paper on the table. Cummings was reading it slowly.

"Don't touch that paper," the deputy ordered sternly. "I might attach it for evidence."

Cummings answered acidly, "It is just an order from Cord Demingway to bury his old pard, and he left a hundred dollars to pay for it."

"So it was Ace Fleming who did for Pete," the deputy said softly. "I better have a talk with that gambler. I don't stand for anyone taking the law into their own hands!"

"That's between you and Ace," Cummings said. "But if I was you I'd be diplomatic about it. Ace can outshoot and outfight you, and we both know it."

"I don't know any such thing!" Saint John shouted.

"Mind your manners, law-dog," Cummings advised. "I don't hold with killing, as you know, but you don't know either side of the story yet. Hold judgment until you know for sure."

"Don't tell me how to do my law work," Saint John said angrily. "Hold up your right hand; I deputize you as part of a posse to bring in the killer!"

Gospel Cummings shook his head. "I'm not the law, which is why I've lived back here as long as I have. On top of that, Ace Fleming is a friend of mine!"

"He killed a man!" Saint John shouted.

"Did you see him kill the deceased?"

"Are you a lawyer?" the deputy countered.

"No, and neither are you, so don't get high and mighty with me. You'll find a bottle under my bunk. Drink hearty."

The burly deputy picked up the bottle, unstopped it, and drank deeply. He passed the bottle to Cummings, who cleaned the neck by plopping a finger in the opening. Cummings turned his back, made a mark with his thumb, and drank down past the mark.

"Just a suggestion," Cummings said quietly. "Never mind Ace Fleming; you can see him any time. Better take after Cord Demingway. He's wanted by the law in seven states."

"Good idea," Saint John agreed. "No one in these parts can read sign like you, Gospel. Take on to side me as special deputy, and we will leave at daybreak for the mesas."

"My business is here," Cummings refused slowly. "I've been paid to read the service for Pete Lagrue, and I've already spent part of the fee. Some other cowboy—not me."

"Afraid mebbe," the big deputy taunted, but he got no rise from Cummings. "The years are slowing you down," Saint John added.

"It might be like you say," Cummings said agreeably. "All of which don't buy you any free heroes to help you do the work you get paid to do. You might try to raise a posse on Ace Fleming's Circle F."

"Reminds me I've got to see Fleming," the deputy remarked. "Like as not he will be running the games up at the Casino."

Gospel Cummings sighed as he sat down at his table. He opened the Book and began to read slowly, savoring the words of wisdom which had come down through the ages. Once he slightly raised his head, and then went on with his reading.

He showed no surprise when a rough voice spoke suddenly from the open door. "Elevate, you old sin-buster. Get them dew-claws ear-high before I bust a cap!"

"Enter in peace, Demingway," Cummings said calmly. "I was expecting you after the law cleared out."

"You're a liar!" the outlaw contradicted him flatly. "You thought I was back on the mesas."

Cummings turned slowly and studied his visitor. Cord Demingway was a cowboy gone wrong. Six feet tall, a hundred and seventy pounds, wolf-lean, and on the prod. He held one of a pair of six-shooters in his right hand.

"I was right outside under that window," he boasted. "Heard every word you and the Saint said. Good thing you refused to take that law badge."

Cummings nodded as he stared at the spare gun in the tall outlaw's left holster. He could see five notches whittled on the cedar handles; there were probably as many more on the meat-gun Demingway held in his steady right hand.

"I wouldn't have read the sign that away," Cummings said slowly. "The way you tell it now, you got those notches by sneaking up and shooting your victims in the back. A man doesn't usually do that who has what you might call gun-pride!"

Cord Demingway's finger tightened on the trigger. "Unsay them words!" he ordered. "Or I'll—"

"You'll prove I was right," Cummings finished for him. "I said to enter in peace, so you can holster your weapon. What did you want to see me about?"

Demingway smiled coldly and controlled his wrath. "I've heard a lot about you, Cummings," he said slowly. "Aside from roosting just outside this skull-orchard like a buzzard, waiting for a chance to pick up some easy money, you've got a rep for minding your own business."

"Which I was doing when you came a-busting in on me," Cummings reminded him. "You've got something on your conscience, so unload it and ride off."

"You stay away from that gold mine," Demingway ordered harshly. "Did you say anything to Ace Fleming?"

Cummings made no pretense of innocence. He knew the badlands better than any working cowhand in and around Vaca. He knew that he had been seen the day he had almost stumbled on the workings deep in the badlands on Circle F graze. He shook his head slowly.

"I figured that was the first honest work those gunhawks had done in years," he answered, "sluicing out pan-gold from the waters of Lost River. How much of a share do they get?"

"Share and share alike, with me taking two shares by right of discovery," Demingway answered without evasion. "Like you told the Saint, I'm wanted in seven states. Word came back from Kid Curry down in South America that a man with a little dinero can live there like a king. I might go for a look."

"How long will it take your boys to clean out that pocket?"

"How'd you know it was a pocket?" Demingway growled.

"I found that claim ten years ago," Cummings answered with a shrug. "I wasn't cut out for shovel-work."

"Now it's different," the outlaw said slowly. Pete Lagrue was my *segundo*, my saddle pard. Ace Fleming killed him!"

"Ace allowed he caught Pete rustling one of his steers," Cummings answered.

"A man has to eat, and that gambler has plenty," Demingway retorted.

"Now, look, fella," Cummings said patiently. "I never saw the cowman yet who objected to a hungry man getting himself some campmeat. What he does not like is for some free-booter to shoot a steer, cut out the steaks and tenderloins, and leave the rest for the varmints. If you'd skinned a carcass, hung the hide up to dry, and packed the meat back to your hide-out, Ace wouldn't have said a word."

"We take what we want," Demingway boasted arrogantly. "It would have been different if Fleming had jumped me instead of Pete."

"No different," Cummings contradicted quietly. "Ace is the fastest gun-hawk in these parts; I've seen him work several times."

"You ever see me work?"

Cummings shook his head. "A man can't do his best fighting when he knows he is wrong," he said slowly.

Demingway spoke up sullenly. "You ever hear of Swifty Matthews?"

"He used to be a Texas Ranger," Cummings answered without hesitation. Said to be double fast with his smoke-poles."

"I had two brothers," Demingway said grimly. "Ace Fleming killed one of them in a poker game over at Silver City. Swifty Matthews killed the other one down at Laredo."

"Ambitious cuss, ain't you?" Cummings asked. "Either one of those two would be enough for most hard cases, but you want to make a clean sweep."

"Which is why I want to live," Demingway answered through tightly clenched teeth. "After that I don't give a hoot!"

"Look," the plainsman said. "No man is entitled to more than a fifty-fifty break in life. Why not settle for Matthews?"

"You mean because both me and him are outside the law," Demingway answered shrewdly. "But I've waited a long time, and it's double or nothing!"

"It's quite a jaunt to Laredo," Cummings suggested. "Further still to the Argentine."

"Matthews is here," Demingway said quietly. "He's looking for Ace Fleming too!"

"Small world, ain't it?" Cummings said, to cover his surprise.

"Matthews wants the mine," Demingway said harshly. "We've killed two of his gun-dogs; he tallied for one of mine."

"Mebbe the Saint does need some help," Cummings said musingly. "Him being what law we have up here in the Strip, and also being in the middle, you might say."

"Tell the law to stay in town, and I'll do his law work for him," Demingway said.

"While I'm running errands, you want to send any money to Boot Hill Crandall?" Cummings asked.

"The Undertaker?"

"That's right. In case Ace smokes you down."

"Tell Crandall not to worry," Demingway said with a wolfish grin. "I'll carry a hundred in gold on me at all times. Tell the law it's open season on star-toters. If he or Fleming wants to send any messages, you'll be safe."

After he had gone, Gospel Cummings turned down his lamp. He stretched slowly to his feet, and his big hands were trembling. He reached to a shelf behind a small curtain, took a flask he kept for emergencies, and raised the bottle to his bearded lips. He followed with a quick chaser of the same, wiped his bearded lips with the back of one hand, blew down the lamp chimney, and made ready for sleep.

## CHAPTER TWO

A tall slender rider drew rein in front of the Cummings cabin, swung to the ground, and tied his sorrel with trailing reins. Gospel Cummings studied the cowboy with critical eyes, noted the double-cinched saddle, tie-fast catch-rope, and heavy bull-hide chaps.

"Howdy, Texas-man," he greeted the young stranger. "Riding far?"

"Vaca town," the cowboy answered, and his voice was a crisp drawl. "I'm looking for Ace Fleming; you might know him."

"Know him well," Cummings answered. "Ace runs the Casino in town, and the Circle F spread out about seven miles."

"Name's Charley Compton," the stranger introduced himself. "You'll be Gospel Cummings."

"Light and stay for grub," Cummings invited cordially. "I've got a deer hung out back."

He watched Charley Compton strip his saddle gear, noting the sure deft movements of the cowboy's hands. Compton also wore a six-shooter thonged low on his right leg, standard equipment in the high Arizona Strip.

"You looking for work?" Cummings asked carelessly.

"You might say I am," Compton answered.

"John Saint John is the law here," Cummings said slowly. "He's looking for a good fast deputy."

"I could get around that way," Compton said after a pause. "What will he pay?"

"Seventy-five a month and cartridges," Cummings answered. "He's a domineering so-and-so."

"I can take orders," Compton said shortly. "Any

trouble in these parts?"

"Trouble is due to start soon," Cummings offered sagely. "Seems like there are two outlaw gangs holed up back in the badlands, and they are gunning for each other. They are also gunning for Ace Fleming. Mebbe you'd like a riding job with Ace better."

"These owl-hooters," Compton said carelessly. "Is one of them Swifty Matthews?"

"You got a grudge to settle?"

"I might have. Who's the other one?"

"Cord Demingway," Cummings answered. "Both these long-riders are fast and accurate with their hardware. How about you?"

"I'm twenty-four, and I'm still alive," Compton answered with a trace of youthful pride.

"Being a Texan, you started doing cow-work about the time you could ride good," Cummings said. "I'm a Texan myself, or I was."

"How far is this place they call Dog Town?"

"Three miles east of Vaca. But better stay away from Dog Town," Cummings advised. "Romance comes pretty high in that den of iniquity."

"You a sky pilot?" Compton asked with a grin.

"I am not a man of the cloth," Cummings answered quietly.

"So I'll ride over to Dog Town when I get hooked up with a job," Compton answered. "Have you seen Matthews?"

"Not in town," Cummings answered. "But if he knows you, chances are he knows you've arrived. He's got three-four hard cases in his gang; Demingway has as many more."

"Thanks, old-timer," Compton answered. "When do we start gnawing on that deer you mentioned? I missed breakfast this morning."

They were finishing the ample meal when Saint John rode down and tied up at the rail. The sun was straight overhead to mark high noon, and the deputy came into the cabin and sniffed.

"There's a plate-full left," Cummings said with a frown. "Deputy Saint John, meet Charley Compton from Texas. He might be interested in a deputy job with you."

"Howdy, Compton," Saint John acknowledged the introduction. "If you are just another yearling saddle-tramp riding through, I wouldn't be interested. Are you?"

"I've been a saddle-tramp, and I'm interested," Compton answered crisply. "I can read sign with the best, shoot fairly accurate, and come out fairly fast. What more do you want for seventy-five a month and shells?"

"Salty hair-pin, ain't he?" the deputy appealed to Cummings. "I'll think it over while I iron the wrinkles from my belly. Do you expect to live forever?"

"Would I be looking for a law job if I was?" Compton countered.

"I can read sign myself," the deputy answered. "Forget about the girl back home who threw you down. There are plenty more."

Compton tilted his head well back to stare up into the big law officer's face. His lips opened as though he were about to make a sharp retort, and then he controlled his emotions.

"We were talking about a job," he said quietly. "I don't need any advice about my romantic interests."

"That's one of the first things you would have to learn," Saint John said patronizingly. "To take orders without question, and keep your mouth shut."

"Go to blazes," Compton said quietly. "I wouldn't work for you at double the wages."

"You never will learn, Saint," Cummings said wearily. "You paw and beller about needing reliable help to do your law chores. Free or for pay, you have to ride roughshod over any one who offers to give you a hand."

Saint John flushed with anger, and stared at Charley Compton for a long moment. "Where did you say you were from?" he asked.

"I didn't say," Compton answered tartly.

"Stranger, or looking for a law job, I'd have to know your background," Saint John said gruffly. "Texas boy, ain't you?"

"That's right, and Texas is a mighty big place," Compton answered. "You say I could like as not find

Ace Fleming at the Circle F?" he asked Cummings.

"Look, son," the deputy said sternly. "There's two owl-hoot outfits operating in these parts. You seem to know them both. You just might be a member of one or the other, and I'll keep an eye on you for a while."

Charley Compton smiled with undisguised amusement. "You sure are going to be busy," he commented. "Watching the Demingway gang, Swifty Matthews, and me. Off-hand I'd say you will need quite a bit of help, and off-hand again, I'd say you are going to have a time finding that help. You don't mind now, I'll be riding along minding my own business."

"You'll sit right there until you answer my questions," Saint John blustered. "Or I'll place you under arrest for suspicion!"

"Suspicion of what?" Compton asked slowly.

"I haven't made up my mind yet," Saint John said. "But it could be two or three things."

Charley Compton half-turned, his right hand flashed down with unbelievable speed, and before he could move, John Saint John was looking into the muzzle of a Peacemaker forty-five.

"Name just one," Compton said quietly. "If it has any merit, I'll surrender for questioning, but you can't bully me worth a damn!"

"That sounds fair enough to me," Gospel Cummings interrupted with a smile. "What's the charge, deputy?"

Saint John sputtered and then looked past Compton. "Ace Fleming coming," he said suddenly. "Ace will help the law!"

"Think up a new one," Compton said, and then he cocked his head to listen. He swiveled his head to stare briefly up the road leading to town, holstered his weapon when he saw a little man coming on a big horse, and hooked both thumbs in his belt.

Ace Fleming rode into the little yard, a picture of sartorial elegance. The gambler wore tailored clothing, handmade boots, and a beaver Stetson. He also wore a brace of six-shooters thonged low on his legs, and an air of competence.

"You need any help to do your law work?" he asked Saint John.

"Ace, make you acquainted with Charley Compton from Texas," Cummings spoke up. "Charley, make you used to Ace Fleming, boss of the Circle F. He just refused to work for the Saint," Cummings added.

"I could use a good gun-hand," Fleming said slowly. "I'll top the law by ten dollars a month and found."

Charley Compton swallowed noisily. "How do you know I'm not an outlaw?" he asked, with a grin at the deputy.

"I can read sign some," Fleming answered. "You're hired, and what you did in your past is your own business."

"Boss, you've hired a man," Compton said soberly.

"I'll try to earn my pay."

He watched Saint John as he spoke. After that exhibition of speed, Saint John made no attempt to get at his holster.

"Are you resisting arrest?" he asked sternly.

"Not if you have some charge," Compton answered quickly. "But if you arrest me, and are wrong, I'll sue the pants off you, and I've got two witnesses!"

"I'll know where to find you," Saint John said with a shrug.

"Swifty Matthews is here, and he's gunning for you, Ace," Cummings interrupted. "Seems like Charley knows both Matthews and Demingway, but I'd like to tell him one thing when he starts hunting."

"Thou shalt not kill," Fleming quoted softly. "That it?"

"Right," Cummings growled. "With his speed, he don't have to ride around killing his fellow humans!"

"I never learned to throw off my shots, when a man is gunning for me," Compton said stiffly.

Fleming looked at Saint John. "It's always open season on hobos and outlaws. You haven't had any howling success running down Cord Demingway and his gang, and they've been here two years. If I can't get any help from the law, I don't want any interference. Do I make myself clear?"

"You can't talk to me as if I were one of your hired hands!" Saint John flared angrily.

"Don't bet I can't," Fleming answered smoothly. "I help pay your wages, and I expect something for my taxes. When I don't get that something, I help myself. You ready to ride, Compton?"

Gospel Cummings listened with a smile on his bearded face. It was an old story to him; Saint John always antagonized those he needed most.

"Thanks for a mighty fine bait of grub, Gospel," Compton said earnestly. "I'll give some thought to what you said."

Compton rode west and north with Ace Fleming, and when they were over the rise, the gambler spoke curiously.

"What do you know about Cord Demingway?" he asked.

"He's an outlaw," Compton said slowly. "A gambler killed his brother Jim over in Silver City back a few years."

Ace Fleming turned abruptly in the saddle. His dark eyes probed at Compton's face, and then the gambler smiled.

"Yeah, I killed Jim Demingway," he admitted. "He tried to run in two extra Aces in a game of draw, but they didn't help his hand much. What's between Demingway and Matthews?"

"Swifty Matthews killed Joe Demingway down in Laredo," Compton answered carelessly.

"You've been a lawman," Fleming said carelessly,

and now it was Compton who whipped about in his saddle.

"You're guessing," he said lightly.

Fleming shook his head. "It always leaves a mark on any man who rides behind a law star," he stated frankly. "It always shows up when gun-play begins. A lawman has to give every man a chance. Now me, I'm a Texan like yourself, but my old Dad taught me years ago never to shuck my six-shooter unless I meant to come out shooting!"

"You've got me there," Compton admitted. "But Saint John is a good lawman the way I read his brands and ear-markings. Overbearing and arrogant, but he don't lack none for sand."

"That's the Saint," Fleming agreed. "Why didn't you sign on with him?" he asked curiously.

"He got to giving me advice, and asking too many questions," Compton answered shortly.

"About the Circle F," Fleming changed the subject abruptly. "You'll ride the wide circles for a while until you learn the range. We'll eat you in the kitchen, and sleep you in the bunkhouse with the other Circle F hands."

"Suits me fine, boss," Compton answered with a smile. "I'll try to earn my pay."

"You will," Fleming said quietly. "Did the Saint tell you to stay away from Dog Town?" he asked.

"Him and old Gospel both," Compton answered

with a growl.

"Another thing, Compton. I saw you draw, and you are plenty fast shedding leather. Gospel Cummings is faster!"

"The devil you whisper!" Compton burst out.

"Simmer down," Fleming said soothingly. "Gospel can call his shots, but I don't believe he ever killed a man. He's ruined several so they will never work at their trade any more, but he don't hold with killing.

"He's got something the rest of us don't have," Fleming continued, and his tone was almost reverent. "He lives by the Book, except for his one fault, which bothers no one but himself."

They were now on hilly graze, and Compton studied the white-faced cattle wearing the Circle F brand on the left hip. A shot blasted faintly from a high ridge. A rider waved his hands and hit his horse with the hooks to disappear down the far slope.

"What you make of that, boss?" Compton asked curiously. "He trying to give us a message?"

"Let's ride yonderly," Fleming answered, and touched his thoroughbred with a blunted spur.

Both were cautious as they climbed the slope to rimrock. Charley Compton reined in and pointed at a forked stick. A piece of paper was fastened to the stick, which was set in a crack of the rock.

Ace Fleming rode close and took the paper. It was written with a stub pencil in a neat flowing hand.

"Listen to this!"

> *"Fleming: If Matthews don't whittle your notch, the undersigned will cut it. Tell Compton to ride back to Texas or else!*
> *Demingway"*

"He's a man of few words," the gambler remarked. "He knows you?"

"Seems as though," Compton answered vaguely.

"You didn't ride up here just to hunt glory," Fleming said bluntly. "Do you want to tell me?"

"No," Compton replied.

Fleming shrugged. "In due time," he murmured. "I want you to meet a salty hairpin I've got on my payroll. Boy by the name of Skid Yancey. First name is Skidmore, about five foot and a half, don't weigh more than a hundred and thirty. If you just have to ride over to Dog Town, take Skid along."

"Down, boss!" Compton said suddenly, and he threw himself sideways from the saddle. He clawed a Winchester from the saddleboot as a flat report echoed from down the slope, and the hat flew from Ace Fleming's head. Charley Compton levered a shell into the breech as he fined his sights, and he squeezed off a slow shot that set the horses to spooking.

Ace Fleming rode into the trail-side brush, stared down the slope, and then put his horse into a dead run. He was staring down at a man in the short grass when Compton galloped down the slope and slid his horse to a stop.

"Nice shooting, Charley," Fleming praised quietly. "You've earned your pay."

Compton emptied his saddle and knelt beside the wounded man. The man's eyes fluttered open for a moment to stare at Compton's tanned face.

"The boss will tally for that one, Charley," he said weakly. "I was shooting at that tinhorn!"

Ace Fleming stared at the stricken man with no emotion on his smooth features. "You know this buscadero?" he asked.

"Name of Jud Thompson," Compton answered tonelessly. "I worked on a spread with him down in Texas for a while. He's one of the Demingway crowd, so it must have been him who left that message."

"You got anything to say before you cash in your chips?" Fleming asked the wounded man.

"Money in hip pocket," Thompson murmured weakly. "Funeral, and a fee for that ornery old sin-buster. I'll see you both in hell!"

"What's he mean, funeral?" Compton asked Fleming.

"Demingway started it when he left a hundred dollars in Gospel's cabin to pay for the burial of Pete Lagrue," he said slowly. "He paid Gospel twenty dollars to read the service. Look in Thompson's wallet pocket."

Charley Compton reached gingerly under the body.

His hand came out holding six double eagles.

"A hundred and twenty in gold," he whispered.

"One of us will have to take him back to town," Fleming said. "I better do it, account of Saint John." He looked up when hoofs rattled down the slope, and a slender rider roared down and slid his lathered mount to a stop.

"Howdy, boss," he greeted Fleming. "You need any help with this pilgrim?"

Charley Compton grinned as he studied the small cowboy. He knew Skid Yancey from Fleming's description.

"Skid, meet Charley Compton, the new Circle F hand," Fleming said quietly. "This hombre had me under his sights, but Charley saw him just in time. Charley got him with his long-gun from up on the ridge."

"That's different," Yancey grunted in a deep bass voice, and he offered his right hand to Compton. "Welcome to our midst, Texas feller," he said cordially. "That's right fair shooting on any man's range."

"Thanks, pard," Compton murmured, and he was surprised at the strength of Yancey's grip. "You must have been stalking that messenger."

"Wait a spell," Yancey said slowly. "I didn't see you; you didn't see me. Now you better talk fast, and tell it straight."

"Lay your hackles, Skid," Fleming said soothingly.

"We both saw that rider of Matthews'. He fired a shot to attract our attention, and then high-tailed over the rise. We rode up here, found a message he left, and I was reading it when this gunny fined his sights on me. How about you taking the late Jud Thompson back to Vaca town?"

"Anything you say, Ace," Yancey growled.

"Take this money along," Fleming said, and handed Yancey the gold pieces. "A hundred for Crandall, and twenty for Gospel Cummings. Notify Saint John, and then get back to the Circle F."

"Like you said, boss," Yancey answered, and gathered up the bridle reins to lead the outlaw's horse. "I'll see you tonight, Charles," he told Compton.

"There's a good hand," Fleming said to Compton. "His worst fault is women, but that's his own business."

"Not more than twenty-five," Compton guessed.

"Twenty-six, and guts of the devil," Fleming answered. "Knows every gal in Dog Town, and lights out for there every pay day."

"They mounted their horses, scanned the skyline carefully and rode across Circle F graze. Neither mentioned the dead man, but Ace Fleming studied the written note several times.

"Demingway could have been an artist," he said slowly.

"He is," Compton spoke up. "With a six-shooter. You ever meet him?"

Fleming shook his head. "I met his brother Jim like you heard," he answered. "He might do some of my fighting for me," he continued with a smile. "Matthews killed his brother, Joe."

They came to the Circle F headquarters and rode into a big neat yard. Fleming pointed out the bunk house, and introduced Compton to a pretty young woman who came from the comfortable ranch house to meet him.

"Sandra, this is Charley Compton, our new hand. Compton, my wife."

"Howdy, Mrs. Fleming," Compton answered shyly.

"Welcome to the Circle F, Charley," Sandra Fleming greeted the cowboy cordially. She frowned as she noticed his tied-down holster. "Fighting pay?" she asked Fleming.

The dapper gambler nodded. "Two outlaw gangs are preying on Circle F beef," he said. "I mean to stop it if I can!"

"I'll take my soogans to the bunk-house," Compton excused himself, and rode to a long low building at the rear.

"He's just a boy, Ace," Sandra Fleming told her husband.

"Don't let that baby face fool you," Fleming warned. "Compton is twenty-four, and he's been around. He saved my life this morning." And he told her about the attempted bush whacking.

## CHAPTER THREE

Skid Yancy rode slowly down the long gradual slope which terminated at Three Points, and Hell's Half Acre. Gospel Cummings came to his cabin door and frowned when he saw the pack horse and its grisly burden. He waited until the slender Circle F cowboy rode up to the rail and dismounted.

"Don't leave the deceased here yet," he cautioned Yancey. "Yonder is the road to Vaca, and Boot Hill Crandall."

"Keep your boots on, Gospel," Yancey answered tartly. "You'll get him back down here in due time. The deceased left some money for you to read his service."

He took a twenty-dollar gold piece from his vest pocket, and flipped it to Cummings who caught it expertly.

"A hard dry road from the Circle F," Cummings said quietly. "Come in and have a bit of something."

"I was hoping you'd ask me, Gospel," Yancey admitted frankly. "She's all of three days till pay day, and me dry as Goose Crick in drought time. Don't mind if I do."

He followed Cummings into the cabin and took

the bottle the old plainsman proffered. After a long hearty drink, he returned the bottle to Cummings.

"That is what remains of the late Jud Thompson out yonder. He put a slug through Ace Fleming's 5 X beaver, but the new hand saw the sheen of sun on his rifle barrel, and squeezed off one shot."

"You mean young Charley Compton?" Cummings asked. "He allowed he might throw off his shots."

"At better than two hundred yards with a long-gun, he didn't noways have time," Yancey explained. "Thompson talked a few before he rode on west. Said he had a hundred in his hip pocket to pay Crandall, and also your fee."

"Have one for the road," Cummings invited. "And don't take Charley over there to Dog Town."

Yancey choked as he was drinking, cleared his throat, and started again with his drink. He passed the bottle back to Cummings, tilted his hat acey-deucey, and started for the door.

"A feller has to have some fun," he said slowly. "I'm not riding herd on that Texas boy. See you some more, old-timer."

Yancey climbed his worn saddle and rode up the trail to Vaca. The light was fading when he stopped in front of the adobe jail. Saint John came out and took a long look at the body lying face down on the saddle, and anchored to the horse, ankles and wrists.

"The name of the deceased, place of the killing,

and the name of the killer," he said importantly.

Skid Yancey squinted up at the big deputy. "The name of the deceased is the late Jud Thompson, outlaw, part of the Demingway crowd, and he was kilt on Circle F range by one Charley Compton, late of Texas. Proceed, Your Honor."

"Comical cuss, ain't you?" Saint John asked caustically. "Where was Ace Fleming during the shooting?"

"Ace was the target for this dry-gulching son," Yancey explained. "Jud was a-laying down the hill some two hundred yards, fining his sights on Ace. Charley saw the rifle barrel, yelled a warning, emptied his own kak, and used one slug on the late Jud. You want I should pack him down to Crandall's, and pay the bill in advance?"

"Those are my orders," Saint John said sternly.

Skid Yancey reared back, threw his head back to get a good look at the deputy, and then mounted his Circle F horse. "Law-dog," he said thinly, "you ain't giving me any orders. Take him down there yourself!"

He hit his horse with the hooks and roared down the street before the startled deputy could answer, and took a short cut to the Circle F. It was an hour after supper when he rode into the ranch and remembered the money in his pocket to pay for Thompson's funeral. He off-saddled and turned his weary horse in with the saddle band, hurried to the cook shack, and met Ace Fleming who was just leaving.

"You pay for the funeral?" Fleming asked suspiciously.

"I'm a son of a buck," Yancey murmured. "The boss has turned Clara-buoyant on me. I got into an argument with the Saint, and I rode off with the money in my pocket."

"The word is clairvoyant, and I'm not a mind-reader," Fleming said sternly. "I just happen to know your shortcomings. I'll pay Crandall tomorrow when I ride in."

Yancey turned the money over reluctantly. He had thought some of a quick trip to Dog Town, telling himself he could repay the money on pay day.

"Like you said, boss," he muttered. "A feller can't have no fun on this here treadmill of life."

"Cheer up," Fleming said with a smile. "I want you to ride with Charley Compton tomorrow. Make a wide circle to the badlands, and get an early start. The cooky kept some grub hot for you, so fly at it."

Yancey finished his meal and went to the bunk house. Shorty Benson was mending a bridle, and Long Tom Brady was talking quietly to Charley Compton. They glanced up when Yancey entered, and Compton looked expectantly at Skid's freckled face.

"What did old Gospel say?" he asked.

"Said you might have throwed off your shot to give that sinner time to repent," Yancey said with a grin. "He'll preach you a sermon next time you light down at his place. Seems like I heard somewhere about you being in a big gun-soiree down Texas way a while back."

Compton started and stared at Yancey's guileless face. "Who told you that?" he demanded.

"You know how word gets around on the grapevine," Yancey said carelessly.

"Must have been some other saddle-tramp," Compton grunted. "How about Saint John?" he changed the subject.

"I rode off and left him with the corpse when he started in giving me orders," Yancey replied with a grin. "I even forgot to leave the money for Crandall, but the boss read my mind and took it away from me."

"Good thing he did," Compton said with a chuckle, "or you'd have geared a fresh horse and lit out for Dog Town."

"I was a-toying with the idea," Yancey admitted honestly. "There's a new gal over in one of Pug Jones's places, but she's kinda offish. I don't think she's a percentage gal, and I could change my ways for her."

Charley Compton leaned forward, but he did not

speak. "What's this filly's handle?" Compton asked lazily.

"Mona Belle," Yancey answered promptly. "Does something to a feller, a name like that. Pretty, ain't it?"

Charley Compton's eyes narrowed and his body stiffened. Yancey did not notice, and he continued talking.

"Seems like an old bar-dog name of Stingaree Burke is her uncle or something," Yancey continued. "He keeps an eye on Mona Belle, and he carries a hog-leg under his apron. Mona Belle looks to be about twenty, and pretty as a new red wagon!"

"You better leave her alone," Brady suggested. "I've heard about Stingaree Burke, and when he was younger, he was one of the fastest gun-passers on the border. He must be sixty-odd by now."

"Every bit of that," Yancey agreed. "Silver white hair, a thin white mustache, and straight as a pine."

"What's this filly doing in the Red Rose Saloon?" Shorty asked curiously.

"Singing, is all," Yancey answered. "And man oh man, can she sing!"

He glanced at Compton, narrowed his eyes, and asked bluntly, "Do you know Mona Belle?"

Compton shrugged. "How do I know until I see her?" he answered crossly. "You don't mind, I'll hit the hay and make up some sleep I lost on the trail."

"Yeah, you do that," Yancey answered. "Ace wants you and me to ride a wide circle tomorrow, back to the lavas. And keep up your strength, Texas boy. You and me are riding into Dog Town Saturday night; it just happens to be pay day."

Compton was asleep almost instantly, despite the murmured conversation of the Circle F crew. He awoke with the first rays of the sun, put on his hat, stomped into his boots, and proceeded to dress. The other members of the crew also crawled out of their bunks, but Yancey and Compton were first in the cook shack.

The rest of the crew trooped in for breakfast, and conversation was second to eating. The food was delicious and abundant. Compton finished his hot coffee and rolled a smoke. He walked out with Yancey, who legged it to a large corral with a catch-rope trailing behind him.

"I want that grulla knothead with the Roman nose for my mount," he told Compton. "I'll snare you that mouse-colored gelding with the line-back. Two of the best mountain horses on the spread, and sure-footed as goats."

He made his cast as the milling horses circled past, snared the grulla, and handed the rope to Compton. He took Compton's rope, made a Holly-ann catch to snare the line-back, and they led the two horses out and tied up at the rail.

"Why do they call it Dog Town?" Compton asked abruptly.

"Huh? Because most of the women have dogs, and every dog in the neighborhood knows it," Yancey answered with a grin. "It's a free and easy life over in Dog Town if a gent minds his own business, and has plenty of dinero. Wine, women, and song, and that Mona Belle filly can sure sing."

Compton frowned and tightened his latigo.

"Let's quit the spread," he said. "Time's a-wasting."

"So it is," Yancey murmured. "It's every bit of six o'clock; it will soon be noon, and half the day is gone."

They left the ranch and headed across open range toward the foothills off to the northwest. Yancey was full of questions, but he was also a working cowboy. A man didn't get along too well if he asked too many questions, and he usually got the answers in due time. Yancey nodded; he was content to wait.

"Hossbacker coming," Compton said briefly, and he reached for the Winchester under his left saddle fender. He held the rifle across his knees as he nodded.

"It's Gospel Cummings," he said, as he recognized the stooped shoulders of the tall plainsman. "Wonder what he's doing back here?"

"Gospel knows this back country better'n any cowhand in the Strip," Yancey explained. "That ain't all," he continued. "He can snake his way into a camp without anyone knowing it. Used to live with, and fight the redskins."

"I'd rather have him on my side than against me," Compton confessed. "He's going to give me what-for for the Jud Thompson go-around."

Gospel Cummings rode off the trail into a stand of scrub oak. His right hand went to the tail of his long coat and came out with a quart bottle of Three Daisies. He pulled the cork with strong teeth, tilted back his head, and quaffed a deep draught. When he rode back to the trail, the tremble had left his strong, brown hands.

"Howdy, gents," Cummings greeted the Circle F pair. "I thought you'd be riding this way. Mind if I rub stirrups a ways?"

"She's a free country, Gospel," Yancey answered. "Me and Charley will be proud to have your company."

"You sleep good last night?" Cummings asked Compton.

"Slept like a log."

"Your conscience didn't bother you none?"

"Not a bit," Compton answered gravely. "After all, the first law of life is self-preservation. Thompson shot first!"

"I believe you, Charley," Cummings answered

gravely. "But there's also another law back here; you might call it jungle law."

"Meaning what, Gospel?" Compton asked with a puzzled expression on his face.

"The law of tooth and fang, or an eye for an eye," Cummings explained. "You rubbed out the late and unlamented Jud Thompson. Ace Fleming did for Pete Lagrue. Cord Demingway will even the score, and there are plenty of places back yonder for a sharp-shooter to belly down in the brush. Do I make myself clear?"

Compton nodded. "Like Thompson did," he answered. "We will have to keep our eyes wide open, and our guns close to our hands."

"I can knock off a deer up to five hundred yards, if the wind is right," Cummings said thoughtfully. "That's farther than most men can see."

"I see what you mean," Compton agreed. "So it had something to do with you riding back here to warn me and Skid. We're listening respectful."

Gospel Cummings stroked his luxuriant brown beard. He started to speak, hesitated a second, and then cleared his throat.

"I'm what you might call neutral," he stated slowly. "I see a lot of things I keep to myself. The outlaws know this, and most times they treat me accordingly. But you'd find it sooner or later, with your ability to read sign. I'm talking about the gold mine."

"What gold mine?" Yancey blurted out.

"Cord Demingway's mine," Cummings answered crossly. "It's on Circle F range, but Ace Fleming has never found it. It's a rich pocket, but there's enough to take a man to South America, and set him up in the cow business."

"I don't believe Demingway will ever leave the country," Compton declared flatly. "If that pocket is on Circle F range, it belongs to Ace Fleming."

"Light down and I'll do some picture-writing," Cummings said, and he swung down from the saddle. When the two Circle F cowboys had followed his example, the old plainsman hunkered down and smoothed a patch of ground with his left hand. He picked up a twig, laid out some rough boundaries, and then made a little circle.

"That's the Utah border up near Saint George," Yancey read the crude map. "Yonder is the Lost River Cave, and that snaky sign is the river above ground. Back here is the Circle F headquarters, and we are sitting about here." And he pointed to a spot on the map.

"The gold mine is here," Cummings said, and he indicated a place near the river. "It's this side of the cave," he explained to Yancey. "So don't stumble into a trap."

"Me and my saddle pard thanks you kindly, old-timer," Yancey said gratefully. "I've been past that place many's the time. We'll have to report it to Ace, of course."

"Mebbe not," Cummings said shortly. "I mean Swifty Matthews found out about the pocket. Now if he and Demingway get to fighting among themselves, it would mean just that much less for the law to do."

"How do you know about Matthews finding out?" Yancey asked bluntly.

Gospel Cummings frowned. "I saw a feller just back from Dog Town," he answered reluctantly. "Seems like he heard some talk in one of the saloons, and he told me before he headed south for Texas and the border. He didn't want any part of either Matthews or Demingway, or Pug Jones either, for that matter."

"Smart hombre," Yancey commented. "Where does that leave the Circle F?"

"I figure Matthews will declare war on Demingway for two reasons," Cummings answered. "First, Swifty Matthews killed Cord Demingway's brother Joe down Laredo way, and Cord sent word he's taken up for him. Second, Matthews wants that gold."

"Stay down!" Compton whispered harshly. "Hoss-backers chousing off to the right near that far hog-back!"

Cummings reached for the saddle-bags behind his cantle. He brought out a pair of old field glasses, cupped them to his eyes, and adjusted the focus.

"Four of them," he muttered. "One is Swifty Matthews; the other three are strangers."

"Leave me take a look," Yancey pleaded. "I know a lot of hombres around Dog Town."

Cummings passed the glasses to him, and Yancey took a long look. He cursed softly under his breath.

"I'll be hornswoggled," he said. "One of those fellers is that old bar-dog in the Red Rose Saloon. Name of Stingaree Burke. He's the uncle of Mona Belle, the singer in the Red Rose!"

He glanced carelessly at Compton and stiffened. Charley Compton's nostrils were flaring with excitement, and he was biting down on his teeth.

"You know that old vinegarroon!" Yancey said to Compton. "You know a lot of people and things you ain't saying much about!"

"Pass me the glasses," Compton said in a growling voice, and Yancey handed the glasses to him without question. "Yeah, that's Stingaree," Compton affirmed. "He used to be a card-sharp, and one of the fastest gun-hawks along the border."

"Then you know the girl, too," Yancey barked.

"I've met her," Compton admitted. "That's all I've got to say right now."

"So Saint John was right when he first met you," Cummings remarked sagely. "He told you to forget the girl who throwed you over down home."

"So-o-o," Yancey murmured. "Charley my boy, you

don't stand a chance," Yancey tormented his pard. "I saw Mona Belle talking intimate to Swifty Matthews back at the Red Rose in Dog Town. Fine figure of a man, Matthews!"

Charley leaped and grabbed Yancey by both arms. He vised down with all his strength, then quickly released his grip. Yancey's arms hung helpless at his sides.

"Don't ever hooraw me again about Mona Belle," Compton said in a deep husky voice.

Skid Yancey made a surprising right-about. "Saying I'm sorry, Charley," he admitted manfully. "I'd die for a gal like Mona Belle, and I'm offering you any help I can give. Here's my hand on it, if I can raise my right arm!"

The two shook hands and stared hard at each other's faces. Charley Compton was the first to smile, a shamed little twisted grin.

"Sorry I man-handled you, Skid," he murmured. "I take it kindly, and a man couldn't ask for a better pard to side him. Yeah, I know Mona Belle, but I don't know why she came up here. That's the Gospel truth!"

"Than which there is no whicher," Cummings murmured solemnly. "Let's ride up a bit closer and see what we can see, now that you boys have decided to be friends."

## CHAPTER FOUR

Charley Compton stared fixedly through the old field glasses. Swifty Matthews was pointing the lead like a man who knew where he was going, closely followed by the other three horsebackers. Gospel Cummings broke in on Compton's thoughts.

"They are heading toward Lost River Cave," he said positively. "I wonder why old Stingaree Burke is so interested?"

"I wonder?" Compton repeated. "He must know something that Cord Demingway does not."

"The way I see it, that go-around yonder is a private fight," Cummings said slowly. "It is none of our put-in, and we'd only be in the middle."

Skid Yancey twisted uneasily. "It's on the boss's land," he argued loyally. "And Ace Fleming pays me my wages."

"Did you ever see two hawks fighting over a rabbit?" Cummings asked. "They fight and rage, and one of them drives the other away. The winner takes the meat and starts for home. Up in an old dead tree an eagle has been watching this whole business. He takes off with a rush, attacks the winning hawk, makes it drop the rabbit, and the eagle then satisfies his hunger."

Yancey stared at the gaunt plainsman, and a grin broke across his freckled face. "I see what you mean, Gospel," he conceded. "We can let those two owl-hooters fight each other, and then Ace can step in to make medicine with the winner."

"Ace, or the law," Cummings corrected. "Sting-aree Burke is after something more than that gold dust Demingway is washing out."

He spoke slowly, watching Charley Compton's face carefully. Compton lowered the glasses and handed them to Cummings. He merely nodded his head.

Rifle-fire broke out across the foothill graze, continued savagely for a few minutes, and then died away. Three horsemen rode back the way they had come, and one of them was leading the fourth horse by the bridle-reins. A man was lying face down in the saddle, and Skid Yancey chuckled without mirth.

"There comes another case for Gospel," he said knowingly. "And it isn't Stingaree or Matthews. What will we do now, Gospel?"

"Stay down," Cummings warned softly. "Yonder comes the law to meet Matthews, and Saint John allows he is big enough to take care of himself."

They watched the tall blocky deputy ride out to intercept the three men. One of the three cut away from his companions and spurred his horse toward the east.

"That's Swifty Matthews," Compton said, after a

hasty glance through the glasses. "He's leaving Burke to do the explaining."

"I reckon it's safe to take a pasear over there now," Cummings said. "But remember; none of us will serve in a posse."

They left the little wallow and rode at an angle toward Saint John who was riding to intercept Burke and his companion. The deputy reached the group first, but he had seen Cummings and his companions riding up for a meet.

"Stop in the name of the law!" the deputy commanded loudly.

Stingaree Burke reined in and faced his horse toward the towering peace officer. Cummings and his companions reached there at the same time, but none of the three spoke. Saint John would do the talking, and he was glaring at Stingaree Burke.

Burke might have been a cavalry officer from his erect appearance. His age was past sixty, but he was straight as a pine, and carried himself with quiet dignity.

"The name is Burke, officer," he said to Saint John. "We were riding for our health, when we were attacked by bandits hiding over by that little stream. Tom Jenkins was killed by bushwhack lead, and we were taking him back to town."

Saint John whipped about in the saddle to face Cummings. "Did you rannies do for the deceased?"

he demanded.

"Use your head for something beside a peg to hang your hat on, Saint," Cummings growled. "You saw the direction we came from."

"Are you Gospel Cummings?" Burke asked.

"The same, and you must be Stingaree Burke."

"Correct, and I'm glad to meet you," Burke answered. He gave no sign that he recognized Charley Compton, but he nodded to Skid Yancey.

"Stingaree is a bar-dog over in Dog Town, Saint," Yancey explained. "He ladles up the forked lightning in the Red Rose."

Stingaree Burke nodded and smiled. "I never touch strong drink myself," he said. "My weakness is gambling."

"Enough of this palaver," Saint John said sharply. "Who do you think dry-gulched Jenkins?"

"We never saw them close up," Burke said hesitantly. "I really couldn't say."

"Just a minute, Burke," Saint John interrupted. "I recognized Swifty Matthews dogging it away from the law. A man is usually known by the company he keeps."

"So that makes my companions all barkeepers," Burke said with a smile.

"Don't cloud the sign," Saint John said sternly. "I demand to know what you were doing out here with Matthews?"

"I refuse to answer on the grounds that I might incriminate myself," Burke said politely. "And I am signing no complaints. Just tell the Coroner that Tom Jenkins came to his death from gunshot wounds at the hands of a person or persons unknown!"

"Don't tell me how to do my law work!" the deputy bellowed.

"Sorry," Burke murmured. "I doubt your authority to question me without a warrant on some specific charge."

"Prairie lawyer, ain't you?" Saint John sneered.

"I was an attorney at one time. But that was many years ago."

"I'll be blamed," Yancey ejaculated. "Stingaree was a law-sharp!"

"Who is your young friend, Skid?" Burke asked.

"Thought you two knew each other," Yancey answered. "Charley Compton, make you acquainted with Stingaree Burke. Stingaree; Charley."

"Howdy," Compton said slowly.

"Glad to know you, Compton," Burke answered. "Texas man, are you not?"

"That's right," Compton replied.

Gospel Cummings listened with his head cocked to the side. A puzzled expression appeared in his deep-set brown eyes, but he remained silent.

Burke reached out and handed the bridle reins of the lead horse to Saint John. "As the law, I turn over the body to you, Mister Deputy," he said politely.

"I'll pay for his funeral, and a fee for Mister Cummings if he will be so kind as to read a service for the departed."

"Mebbe you better ride into Vaca with me as a material witness," Saint John growled.

"You can find me any time at the Red Rose in Dog Town," Burke answered. There is nothing I can add to what I have already told you."

"Just a minute," Saint John said bluntly. "Who's this other hombre with you?"

"Tim Kelly," Burke answered for his companion. "He works for Pug Jones, dispensing hospitality at the Silver Dollar Bar."

"Happy to meet you," Kelly said to Saint John. "I was just an innocent bystander."

The deputy looked down at the rifle in Kelly's scabbard. "You've been smoking that long-gun!" he accused him.

"That's right," Kelly admitted. "What would you do if outlaws attacked you from the bresh? Howdy, Yancey."

"Howdy, Kelly. Did you tally for any of Demingway's outfit?"

"Who's this Demingway character?" Kelly asked innocently.

"You better give up, Skid," Cummings advised. "Kelly refuses to answer on advice of counsel. Right, Burke?"

Stingaree Burke holstered his weapon smoothly,

reached into a vest pocket, and handed Cummings six pieces of gold. "Thank you, Cummings, and I'd take it kindly if you would pay for the services for the late Tom Jenkins," he said quietly. "You can find me at the Red Rose any time you want me, Saint John," he told the deputy, and reining his horse with a nod at Kelly, the two rode eastward.

Saint John watched them go with his mouth open, and nothing to say. Skid Yancey stared at the dead man on the saddle and spoke to Charley Cummings.

"Three will get you five that one will get Saint John two," he said cryptically.

"I hope you are wrong," Cummings said quickly. "There has been enough killing."

"Tim Kelly is one of the best rifle shots in these parts," Yancey explained. "When he smokes his long-gun, there's meat on the table!"

"Meaning he like as not got one of Demingway's crowd?" Charley Compton asked.

Yancey nodded. "I've seen Tim shoot," he admitted. "He can shoot the eye from a snake at a hundred yards, and call which eye!"

"I'll ride back to town with you, Saint," Cummings offered. "These two Circle F hands have their own work to do."

"We'll tie this horse up and ride over to Lost River first," Saint John said curtly.

"Not me," Cummings refused. "And you make a

mighty big target your ownself."

"I'm rodding the law in these parts!" Saint John shouted. "You'll do it the way I say!"

Gospel Cummings gathered up his bridle reins. "Well, it was nice meeting you again, Saint," he said quietly. "You go your way, and I'll go mine."

"Me and Charley will go ours," Yancey added. "So long, gents!"

John Saint John was left in the clearing holding the reins of the led horse. He glared savagely in two directions, and then called gruffly to Gospel Cummings.

"Hold up a spell, you old sin-buster. I'll ride in with you!

"I ain't satisfied none about that Stingaree Burke," Saint John growled. "I'm going to ride over there to Red Dog one of the days soon, and have a long talk with that old son."

"Better talk soft," Cummings advised. "Did you notice the way he skinned the leather off that old smoke-pole of his?"

"This country is getting lousy with fast gun-hawks," the deputy complained. "I ain't satisfied about that young Charley Compton, either."

"You didn't like Ace Fleming for the same reason when he first came here," Cummings reminded him. "Not forgetting Skid Yancey, Swifty Matthews, and Cord Demingway."

"That's what I mean," Saint John complained. "Boot Hill will be filled up before this ruckus is over, and I don't even know what it's all about."

"That's the pity of it," Cummings agreed sadly.

They rode along in silence for a time, started down the long slope to Three Points, and Saint John growled as he pointed toward a horse tied at the rail near the Cummings cabin.

"Another owl-hooter," he said hoarsely. "Like as not the hombre Tim Kelly killed with his rifle."

Cummings swung down, stripped his riding gear, and went to his cabin. He was staring at a paper and some pieces of gold when Saint John entered.

"The deceased is one Sid Simon," Cummings said wearily. "With his funeral paid for in advance."

Saint John walked out and tied to the rail the horse he had led. The deputy mounted as Cummings came to the cabin door.

"I'll send Boot Hill Crandall down with his wagon," he told Cummings. "You will get them back in due time."

"*Vaya con Dios,*" Cummings murmured.

Back on the high trail, Skid Yancey turned to Charley Compton with an eager look in his eyes. "How you fixed for spending money?" he asked hopefully.

"I'm holding a few dollars," Compton answered. "Will twenty be enough?"

"I'll pay you back Saturday," Yancey promised. "Let's circle around and ride into Dog Town. Stingaree Burke wanted to talk to you, and I saw him give you the high sign."

"What high sign?" Compton replied.

"When I introduced you to him," Yancey answered. "I can read sign some. Was he really a lawyer one time?"

"From what I hear, he practiced down in El Paso," Compton said carelessly. "But he has a besetting sin, like he said. With old Gospel it's strong drink, and with Stingaree it's gambling."

Money changed hands before they tightened their cinches for the ride to Dog Town. Yancey tucked the twenty dollars into his vest pocket, rolled a smoke, and flicked a match to flame with a thumb-nail.

"Wait until you hear Mona Belle sing," he said in a hushed voice. "She's like an angel."

"Yeah," Compton agreed. "So just remember that."

"Meaning anything personal?" Yancey demanded instantly.

"Yeah, I do," Compton answered bluntly. "In Texas there are only two kinds of women: good and bad. You were speaking about an angel."

"I could mend my ways," Yancey flared angrily. "And by dogies, I might do it!"

"You'd probably live longer," Compton remarked carelessly, and Yancey stared at him with his shoulders hunched forward.

"I don't understand all I know about this puzzle," he said slowly. "If Mona Belle is all you say she is, what's she doing in a place like the Red Rose over there in Dog Town?"

"What's Stingaree Burke doing there?" Compton countered.

"Hmm," Yancey hawed in his throat. "Whatever it is, it has something to do with Swifty Matthews and Cord Demingway. And whatever it is, two men died this morning because of it."

"More men will die," Compton said briefly. "Let's ride!"

They rode into the sprawling little settlement of Dog Town about three o'clock, entering from the west. A dozen dogs slept in the shadow of low buildings; other dogs barked from the windows of a long low building where each room had a private door from the outside.

"You see that little white cottage down the road, with a picket fence around it?" Yancey asked.

"I see it."

"That's where Stingaree and Mona Belle live," Yancey answered. "Mona Belle only sings in the evening, and she always goes home by ten o'clock."

"You mean she stays in that house alone at night?" Compton asked.

Yancey laughed softly. "Don't try to break in

there," he warned. "Major will chew your hind leg off. That's Mona Belle's dog, a big black brute they call a Labrador retriever."

They tied up at the rack and entered the Red Rose where a score of men were lined up at the bar. A stocky, wide-shouldered man nodded at Yancey, and stared at Compton.

"Pug Jones, meet Charley Compton," Yancey made the introductions. "How's every little thing with you?"

"Tole'able," the saloon man answered with a shrug. "You and your pard staying over tonight?"

"Not all night," Yancey answered. "I'm a working man, remember?"

"So why ain't you working?" Jones asked.

"Look, Pug, I don't ride over here and tell you how to run your business," Yancey said flatly. "So how I do mine is my business."

"You don't have to go on the prod," Jones retorted. "Is your business with Stingaree?"

"My bar business is," Yancey said stiffly. "What in blazes put you on the peck?"

"Tom Jenkins," Jones answered promptly. "He was one of my boys, and now he's kicking up hot ashes in the devil's coal pile!"

"None of us can live forever," Yancey said with a shrug. "Let's cut the trail dust from our windpipes, Charley."

Several of the men along the bar turned to look Charley Compton over. All were gun-hung, roughly dressed, and hard of feature. Compton ignored their direct stares. He nodded at Stingaree Burke, who had just gone on duty behind the long bar.

"Whiskey straight, and leave the bottle," Yancey ordered.

"Small beer for me," Compton said.

"How's Mona Belle?" Yancey asked, as Burke brought the drinks.

"Very well, thank you," Burke answered coldly. "Like you know, she does not receive company."

"Did you tell her Charley was here?" Yancey asked guardedly.

Burke stared at the freckle-faced cowboy, and then answered stiffly. "She already knew it. Mona Belle has nothing to say to Compton."

Charley Compton stared at the beer cupped in his right hand. He turned his head when a hand touched his shoulder.

"You heard Stingaree," Pug Jones said in a low voice. "Stay away from Mona Belle!"

"Keep out of my business, Pug," Burke said quietly.

"It's part of mine, too," the saloon man growled. "Business is twice as good since Mona Belle started singing in the Red Rose, and she lends class to the place. I don't want anything to spoil it!"

Skid Yancey saw that Compton was restraining

himself with difficulty. Compton had not touched his small beer; he just stood rigid with the glass clasped tightly in his left hand.

"Who is this hombre?" Jones asked Burke.

"Compton is a new hand on the Circle F," Yancey answered quickly. "You have to have the history of every cowhand who rides in here to spend his money?"

Charley Compton turned slowly. He stared hard at Pug Jones, who had stepped back with both hands poised above the twin holsters on his thick legs.

"Are you asking for gun-trouble?" Compton asked bluntly.

"Start winging any time you're of a mind!" Jones challenged.

Charley Compton sighed, turned as if toward the bar, and his right hand moved like heat lightning. His gun nozzle was buried in the saloon man's thick middle when Compton swung back again. Pug Jones gasped and elevated both hands ear-high.

"Don't trigger," he whispered. "I talked out of turn!"

"No hard feelings," Compton answered easily, and he removed the pressure and holstered his six-shooter. "But would you mind telling me how I rubbed you the wrong way, Jones?"

"I said I made a mistake," Jones muttered, and he whirled and walked to the far end of the bar near the front entrance.

Skid Yancey stared, poured another stiff drink, and downed it neat. "Let's drift," he said huskily. "Before Pug gets word to his gun-hands. I know the way he works."

Compton threw his beer in the trough in front of the bar. He left the saloon with Yancey, nodded at Pug Jones, and went out to his horse. The two cowboys mounted and rode out of town.

"I wonder what got into Pug?" Yancey asked. "I was watching you all the time; you hardly said a word to him."

"It was what I didn't say that stuck in his craw," Compton said soberly. "Jones is a lot like Saint John in that respect; overbearing and domineering. Other men are supposed to jump when he makes talk, and I don't jump worth a damn!"

"So you're a marked man from now on," Yancey said with a shudder. "Some gunny will lay in the brush and knock you out of your saddle."

"It might be like you say," Compton answered carelessly. "We ought to ride into the Circle F just about grub time."

"Pug is the boss of Dog Town, make no mistake about that," Yancey insisted. "I've seen him kill a man, and cripple two more with his fists. He's a dirty fighter in a dirty business, but he don't lack none for guts."

"I'm sure he doesn't," Compton agreed. "I can say the same thing for Stingaree Burke."

"What you mean by that?"

"Just what I said," Compton answered. "Stingaree has a good reason for being in the Red Rose, but he and Jones don't like each other."

"You wanted to see Mona Belle," Yancey said quietly.

Compton stopped his horse and faced Yancey with a spot on color on each high cheek-bone. "I'm going back to see her now," he said quietly. "I'd prefer to go alone."

"Nuh uh," Yancey negatived the suggestion. "I never dogged it on a pard up to now, and I'm too old to learn new tricks. I know a shortcut up an alley, and I'll stay with the horses while you talk to the girl!"

Compton shrugged. He followed the slender cowboy through a bosque of low trees, turned into an alley and came to a white picket fence. Both men swung down and tied up near the alley, and again it was Yancey who took the lead and opened a small gate.

He knocked at a side door, and a low warning growl came from inside the little house. The door opened a crack, and a girl's voice spoke inquiringly.

"Is that you, Uncle?"

"It's Skid Yancey from the Circle F," Yancey answered promptly. "A friend of yours wants to say hello."

The door opened and a beautiful girl stood framed in the doorway. She smiled at Yancey, and then her dark eyes swung up to see his companion. She gasped as a dog whined eagerly.

"Go away, Charley," the girl said hurriedly. "The answer is still no."

"Don't go riding, Mona Belle," Charley Compton said slowly. "Could I scratch Major's ears?"

The door bounced open suddenly as the dog leaped against it. Then a big sleek dog was jumping on Compton, and it was evident the two were old friends.

"You were a fool to come here, Charley," the girl scolded. "But do come in before you are seen."

Charley Compton opened the door and entered the little house. "You stay with the horses, Skid," he said over his shoulder, and closed the door. Then he turned, and Mona Belle shook her head when Compton opened his arms.

"You saw Uncle Burke?" she asked.

"I saw him," Compton answered. "He said you didn't want to talk to me, so I knew you did."

"Some men are spending gold dust in the Red Rose," the girl whispered. "Pug Jones is getting suspicious."

"I know," Compton answered. "He jumped me not long ago. Why did you come up here?"

"My last name is Courtney, remember," the girl asked.

"I remember," Compton agreed moodily. "I'm at the Circle F if you need me. I better go now."

Mona Belle was of medium height, and superbly made. Her skin was a dusky rose, accentuated by dark hair and eyes. Compton moved quickly, took her in his arms, and kissed her on the lips. Then he stepped away with his head bowed.

"I'd kill any other man in Dog Town who did that," Mona Belle said quietly. "Goodbye, Charley Compton!"

## CHAPTER FIVE

Gospel Cummings filled a wooden tub with water which he heated on his old wood stove. The day was Friday; there would be four services that afternoon in Hell's Half Acre. There was little he could say for the four men who had met a sudden and violent death, but Gospel Cummings would say that little reverently, leaving the judgments to a higher power.

Cummings finished dressing with trembling hands. He glanced through the front window to see that no one observed him. Then he reached for a quart of Three Daisies and made a careful mark with his left thumb. His calculations were in error as always; he drank deeply, and past the mark. But the tremble had left his strong brown hands when he replaced the bottle under the head of his bunk.

Cummings ate a simple meal and washed the few dishes. Then he shrugged into his long-tailed coat, set his best black Stetson firmly on his head, and picked up the Bible from the deal table.

The click of shod hooves turned Cummings' gaze to the sloping trail that led down from the Circle F. His eyes widened when he saw Ace Fleming riding down with his wife, Sandra. Then came Skid Yancey with Charley Compton and Shorty Benson. Cummings remembered that Fleming always attended the services of those he had helped to another world.

Cummings turned to the door when hoofs sounded from the road leading to Vaca. A tall, white-haired man was riding with a remarkably pretty girl. This would be Stingaree Burke, who was flanked on the left by Tim Kelly, bartender in the Silver Dollar over at Dog Town. The girl would be Mona Belle, Burke's niece.

"She is beautiful," Cummings murmured. "With a trace of Spanish blood, unless I misread the signs. I wonder why Burke brought her to the burials?"

He sought solace in a last drink before leaving his cabin. The rattle of wheels told him that Crandall was approaching, this time with two wagons. Saint

John rode ahead of the first black wagon, and the deputy had a Winchester in the saddle-boot under his left leg. John Saint John never left any doubt as to who was the law in the Strip.

Gospel Cummings left the cabin and walked to the entrance of the burying ground. He preceded the first wagon, walking with measured tread to the spot where four graves had been prepared. He took a position at the head of one of the graves and slowly removed his hat. Four Mexican gravediggers waited a respectful distance with their heads uncovered.

Boot Hill Crandall tooled his team expertly, and swung his wagon into position. The driver of the second wagon alighted to help Crandall. They placed the coffins on stakes laid across the graves, and retreated to stand by their teams.

John Saint John dismounted with a flourish.

"You may proceed with the ceremonies, Gospel."

"Thank you," Cummings murmured. "You will please remove your hat."

Saint John complained, but he removed his head gear. Cummings opened the Book and began to read in a low clear voice of remarkable quality. The service was brief; there was no eulogy.

Gospel Cummings left the graves. He walked sedately through the place of the doomed and the damned, but his pace quickened as he neared his cabin. His hand reached for, and found the bottle of whiskey; a hand which was trembling slightly. A hand which was once more steady when Cummings replaced the bottle under his bunk. Then he went out to the tie-rail where the various horsebackers were acknowledging introductions. He heard Charley Compton say: "Mrs. and Mister Fleming, may I present Miss Mona Belle Courtney?"

Sandra went to Mona Belle at once. "I'm so happy to meet you, Miss Courtney."

"Please call me Mona Belle," the girl answered with a flashing smile.

"And you call me Sandra," Fleming's wife agreed. "Please come and stay with us for a visit when you can."

"May I?" Mona Belle asked hesitantly. "Have you met my uncle, Mr. Burke?"

"Charmed, Mrs. Fleming," Stingaree Burke answered gallantly, and he bowed from the waist.

"My husband, Ace Fleming," Sandra continued. "Now we all know each other." And she saw Cummings. "Gospel, I'm so glad to see you," she cried. "You haven't visited me for two whole weeks."

"I am coming soon," Cummings said with a smile. "How is Sugar-Foots?"

"Asking for you every day," Sandra Fleming replied. "That's my two-year-old daughter," she told Mona Belle. "She and Gospel are sweethearts. Her right name is Deloise."

"I've some questions to ask you, Burke," Saint John interrupted importantly.

"Not here," Cummings objected heartily. "This is hardly the time or the place, Saint John!"

"Still telling me how to do my law work," the deputy said coldly, and again he faced Burke. "Just what were you fellows looking for the other day on Circle F range?"

"For that which was lost," Burke answered quietly. "We did not find it. Shall we go, Mona Belle?"

"Just a minute, bar-dog!" Saint John growled. "You'll go when I say you can go!"

"There are ladies present." Charley Compton spoke for the first time since making the introductions. "He and Mona Belle will leave if they are so minded!"

The deputy turned his full gaze upon Compton and raked him savagely with narrowed eyes. "Interfering with an officer in the discharge of his duties?" he asked coldly.

"What duties?" Ace Fleming cut in. "Burke did nothing; perhaps I'm the man you want. Or Charley for instance, or perhaps Tim Kelly. Make up your mind, Saint!"

"You stay out of this!" the deputy roared. "You fellers all be at an inquest to be held in the courtroom in Vaca at three o'clock!"

"We will all be there," Fleming told the towering

deputy. "Won't we, gentlemen?"

Yancey, Kelly and Compton nodded their heads. Sandra Fleming turned eagerly to Mona Belle as Saint John left for Vaca.

"Won't you ride with me to the Circle F?" she invited. "Your uncle can attend the inquest, and pick you up there, unless you will stay a few days."

"I couldn't leave Major," Mona Belle said hesitantly. "That's my Labrador dog, and the best friend I have."

"Shorty will ride back with you and Mona Belle," Fleming told his wife. "This inquest is a mere routine, and won't take long. Everyone is invited for supper, and we will expect you all."

"Thank you heartily, Fleming," Stingaree Burke said with a warm smile. "Mona and I have a day off, but I can't say for Tim Kelly."

"I've got to get back to the Silver Dollar after the doings," Kelly excused himself. "But thanks just the same."

The two women rode away with Shorty Benson. Cummings invited the men into his cabin where they took seats on the bunks. Ace Fleming and Stingaree Burke were studying each other.

"We've several things in common, Burke," Fleming said quietly.

"Gambling," Burke answered promptly. "Name another."

"I could name two, but I won't," Fleming said with a smile.

"Seems as though we both like and respect Charley Compton," Burke said with an answering smile.

"You embarrass me, but thanks just the same," Compton said gratefully. "What's there to these inquests?"

"Routine," Fleming said with a shrug. "No complaints have been signed; the jury will bring in verdicts of justifiable homicide for the record."

"If you have a spare, break it out, and I will replace it, Gospel," Fleming said to Cummings. "These inquests are dry business at best."

Cummings produced a new bottle and handed it to Stingaree Burke, who took a folding corkscrew from a vest pocket. Burke pulled the cork and handed the bottle to Fleming.

"To the confusion of our enemies, if we have any," Burke said quietly.

"I'll drink to that," Fleming answered, and drank sparingly from the bottle.

It went the rounds, with Cummings and Compton abstaining.

"We'd best be riding to Vaca," Fleming suggested. "Old Tom Carr is the Justice, and a sensible man. He won't stand for any usurpation of authority in his court from the Saint."

They left the cabin and walked out to untie and

mount their horses. There was no hurry, and they arrived in Vaca at a leisurely walk.

Judge Carr also ran the general store; now he was in his chambers behind the courtroom. He came out as the men entered, and they all rose to their feet until he had seated himself behind the bench. John Saint John read off the names of the deceased, stated the facts, and suggested that each case be tried separately.

"Nonsense," Carr said testily. "All these hombres were outside the law, and I believe they all shot first. Gentlemen, what is your verdict, or do you want to arrive at same in private?"

"I've been elected foreman, Your Honor," an old cattleman spoke up, as he arose to his feet. "My name is Cal Brighton, of the Box B. We the jury find that the deceased came to their deaths of gunshot wounds, after deliberate provocation. On all and each of them, we render a verdict of justifiable homicide!"

"Gentlemen of the jury, I thank you in the name of the Court and for the County and State," Judge Carr said gravely. "The four deceased were outlaws; the defendants, if any, are acquitted. Court is dismissed!"

John Saint John appeared disappointed; he had lost another opportunity to exercise his authority. Gospel Cummings shook hands with Cal Brighton, and introduced Compton and Burke.

"I've been missing a few cattle lately, Gospel," the old cowman complained irritably. "But then, there are two sets of owl-hooters holing up in the lavas, and I reckon they have to eat." He glanced at the big deputy, and Saint John went on the defensive at once.

"I'll ride out to your place and deputize some of your hands for a hunt," the deputy suggested eagerly.

"You won't," Brighton contradicted. "My boys all know you, and they won't take your domineering orders. When we think the time is right, we'll ride on our own!"

"You can't take the law into your own hands!" Saint John argued loudly.

"You heard the verdict this afternoon," Brighton reminded him. "It looks like we can."

"We better get started for the Circle F," Charley Compton suggested. "It's quite a piece over the hill, and Woo Fong will have supper ready."

They left the courtroom, mounted their horses, and rode out of town. Saint John waved a hand and turned in at the jail. They arrived at the Circle F nearly two hours later, and Ace Fleming straightened in his saddle when a racing horse came out of the big yard in a dead run. Shorty Benson slid his horse to a stop and went straight to Fleming.

"Don't go to fighting your head, boss," he pleaded. "They got Sugar-Foots!"

Fleming's face turned pale. He raced up to the

house, flung himself from the saddle, and ran into the big front room. Woo Fong was lying on a cowskin couch, and Sandra Fleming was bathing the aged Chinaman's head. Woo Fong saw Fleming and sat up weakly.

"Who got Deloise?" Fleming demanded harshly.

Sandra Fleming held back her tears as she arose to her feet. "Woo never saw the man who struck him on the head with a gun," she said quietly. "Deloise was playing in the kitchen; she was gone when Woo regained consciousness!"

"Where's Mona Belle?" Stingaree Burke demanded.

"She raced over to Dog Town to get Major, her dog," Sandra said worriedly. "Mona Belle said that Major could follow any scent!"

"Come on, Compton!" Burke said sternly. "You and I will follow in case she needs any help. Some of you old hands circle for sign!"

Compton hurried outside with Burke; they mounted and roared toward the east at a dead run. There was no opportunity for talk until they reached Dog Town an hour later, and saw Mona Belle's horse tied to the picket fence near the alley.

Mona Belle came out of the house with the big black dog. She had also strapped on a gun-belt. Her pretty face was gravely determined, but she expressed relief when she saw her uncle.

"They took Sandra's little girl," Mona Bell said quietly. "Major will take the trail if they left one."

She mounted her sweating horse without even speaking to Compton. They rode back at a more leisurely pace because of the dog, and it was almost dark when they reached the Circle F. Gospel Cummings met them at the tie-rail with Sandra Fleming.

"There were two of them," Cummings stated positively. "We've held the others back so as not to cloud the sign. Let the dog smell those hoof-prints first."

"Start working, Mona Belle," Burke told his niece. "Major will have to be mighty smart to untangle this one. The bootprints of those two kidnappers, the scent of the horses, and the smell of the little girl."

Mona Belle dismounted and snapped a leash on the retriever's collar. She led him to the rail, pointed out the two sets of hoof-prints, and then led him to the kitchen. Woo Fong had recovered enough to look after his cooking. The big dog smelled the aged Chinese, sniffed about the floor, and raised his head. Mona Belle took a little dress from Sandra and allowed the dog to sniff eagerly. Then she led him back to the tie-rail and again showed him the prints of the two horses.

Shorty Benson had saddled fresh horses. The party quit the ranch and followed the dog who was racing ahead with nose to the ground. The dog stopped suddenly and began to circle in confusion. Mona

Belle watched with a puzzled confusion on her pretty face until Gospel Cummings rode up and spoke quietly.

"They've given Major a forked trail," he explained. "Keep your horses back so as not to cloud the sign. Hold my horse, Skid." And they all watched while Cummings dismounted.

"They separated here," Cummings explained. "One of those owl-hooters rode back toward Lost River; the other headed east. Which one do you want the dog to follow?"

"I've got an idea," Charley Compton said slowly. "It's just a suggestion, but see what you think. Gospel and Ace know that Lost River country inside and out. Skid and Stingaree know Dog Town and that easterly badlands. Put the dog toward the east, and let's split up into two parties."

"That's using your head, Charley," Cummings praised quietly. "You better ride with Burke and Yancey."

The two parties split up immediately, with Shorty Benson complaining because he had to ride back to the Circle F with Sandra. Cummings, Fleming and Yancey took the west trail leading toward Lost River, while Mona Belle put the dog on the tracks leading east. She rode after the dog, with Burke and Compton following at a short distance.

"I've got a hunch, Charley," Stingaree Burke said

quietly. "Looks to me like these tracks are leading right back to Dog Town, and there are a lot of women in Dog Town. Are there any back there at the owl-hoot hideout at Lost River?"

Charley Compton appeared startled. "I believe you are right, Stingaree," he agreed. "That means Sugar-Foots will like as not be with one of the girls who works for Pug Jones!"

"That's the way I figure it," Burke said grimly.

The black dog was coursing ahead strongly, and maintaining a fast trot. When the lights of Dog Town loomed up ahead, Burke called to Mona Belle.

"Better put Major on the leash, Mona Belle!"

The girl stopped her horse and dismounted, and called the dog. He reluctantly left the hot scent and came to her, and she fastened a long leash to his collar. Then she mounted again and held the eager dog in check.

"What do you think, Uncle?" she asked quietly.

"Charley and I believe we will find the baby with one of the girls from the saloon," Burke answered frankly. "If we do, you circle off with Major and stay back!"

Mona Belle nodded and started her horse. Major strained at the leash with little whines of eagerness in his throat. They entered Dog Town, and the dog stopped in front of a door in a long building known as the "Cribs." Mona Belle dismounted and allowed the dog to smell the little dress she took from her belt. Major sniffed the air, put his nose to the ground, and hurried straight for a closed door.

"All right, Mona Belle," Burke said quietly. "Stand back!"

The two men dismounted and anchored their trained cow-horses with trailing reins. Charley Compton stayed at the end of the building while Burke went to the door. Burke knocked on the panel, and for a moment there was silence. Then a woman's voice spoke sharply.

"Who is it, and what do you want?"

"I want to talk some to you, Lilly Mae," Burke answered guardedly. "Stingaree Burke from the Red Rose."

The door opened a crack, and a buxom woman stared at Burke.

"Are you alone?" Burke asked.

"You might say I am. What's it to you?"

"I want my Mommy," a childish voice cried. "I wanna go home!"

"Who is that?" Burke asked sternly. "I didn't know you had a baby, Lilly Mae!"

"Lots of things you don't know, Pop," the woman answered, and she attempted to shut the door.

Burke put his boot in the crack, and the woman reached out and struck at him. He pushed the door open, and was met by the muzzle of a six-shooter against his breast-bone.

"Get out, or I'll lean on the trigger!" the woman threatened. "In this town it's a good thing to mind your own business!"

"Drop that gun, sister," a feminine voice told Lilly Mae. "Stingaree won't shoot a woman, but with me it's different!"

"If it ain't the song-bird," Lilly Mae sneered. "Just go ahead and shoot, Dearie. You might get me, but I'll get old Stingaree!"

She did not hear the back door open from the alley. Charley Compton stepped inside and shouldered into the woman with a quick thrust. Lilly Mae was knocked sprawling, and the gun exploded with a deafening roar. She rolled over and tried to bring the smoking gun to bear on Compton, but Mona Belle pressed trigger and shot the gun from the woman's hand.

Stingaree Burke snatched up the child from a couch and hurried outside. Compton grabbed Mona Belle and rushed her through the door to her horse. The dog was now barking furiously, and Mona Belle mounted and spoke sharply.

"Quiet, Major. Good work, boy!"

Charley Compton mounted his horse and took the child from Burke's outstretched arms. Then they left Dog Town by the alley as men and women came running from every direction. They rounded a corner just as a fusillade of shots roared out, and Stingaree sent the girl ahead with the dog.

Burke whipped out his six-shooter and emptied the gun rapidly, shooting over the heads of several men who were running from the alley. Charley Compton rode fast with the little girl, who clung to him with her chubby arms around his neck.

"I want my Mommy," she whimpered.

"I'm taking you to your Mommy, Sugar-Foots," Compton said.

"Sugar Foots?" the child repeated, and she became instantly quiet. "I want my Uncle Gospel."

"He sent me to bring you, Sugar-Foots," Compton assured the child.

Stingaree Burke rode up fast, reloading his six-shooter. Mona Belle was controlling the eager dog. She spoke jerkily to her uncle.

"I wonder who the men were?"

"I wonder," Burke said grimly. "How bad did you hurt Lilly Mae?"

"Bad enough," Mona Belle said, with a catch in her voice. "I shot her right hand pretty bad, I'm afraid."

"And you saved my life," Compton said gratefully. "What are you going to do with it now?"

"Give it back to you," the girl answered with a smile. "You saved mine one time, remember?"

"Save that chit-chat for another time," Burke said testily. "The way I see it, this ties in with Cord Demingway. I wonder if he and Pug Jones have made a deal?"

"We can't go back there now," Mona Belle said emphatically.

"Stay at the Circle F," Compton suggested. "Sandra says she would be glad to have you."

"There goes my job," Burke said with a sigh.

"I wonder what Skid will say?" Compton murmured.

"Skid Yancey?" Burke repeated. "What's he got to do with it?"

"He kinda liked Lilly Mae," Compton said slowly.

"Pfft!" Burke blew with his lips. "Skid liked all the gals!"

"Yonder's the lights of the Circle F," Compton said suddenly. "You better ride ahead and break the news, Stingaree. I have the little girl, and Mona Belle has the dog, so you can make better time.

Burke touched his horse with a spur and galloped ahead in the darkness. Compton rode closer to Mona Belle with the sleeping child in his arms.

"I love her," he said softly. "I didn't know holding a baby could make me feel like this."

"She loves and trusts you," Mona Belle answered, and her throaty voice was wistfully tender.

"I wish you did," Compton said bluntly.

"Uncle has told the folks," Mona Belle changed the subject quickly, and then they were riding into the Circle F yard.

Sandra Fleming was waiting on the front porch. Compton walked his horse close and leaned over in the saddle.

"She's asleep, bless her," he said softly. "And she is not hurt a bit!"

Sandra Fleming took the baby and kissed her tenderly. "Ace and I will never forget, Charley," she promised.

"You have guests for a while," Compton answered. "Stingaree and Mona Belle cannot return to Dog Town tonight. Mona Belle will tell you about it. Can they stay here?"

"For as long as they like," Sandra answered heartily. "Please come into the house."

"I'll put up the horses," Compton answered. "How's old Woo Fong?"

"He has a headache, but he kept supper warm," Sandra answered.

She went into the house, followed by Mona Belle and her uncle. Woo Fong ran from the kitchen, stared at the child in Sandra's arms, and then came forward on tiptoes. He leaned down and kissed her gently on a cheek.

"Amen," he said happily. "The Big Boss answered Woo's prayers!"

Sandra made a bed for Deloise on the couch, and then sat down to watch the sleeping child. "I'm worried now about Ace and Gospel," she told Burke.

"Stop worrying," Burke said decisively. "That old Injun fighter will know just what to do, and more, what not to do. And offhand I'd say your husband can take care of himself in any kind of a ruckus."

Charley Compton came into the room from the kitchen. "I'm hungry," he said, like a small boy. "When do we eat?"

"Right now, Cholly my boy," a voice said behind him, and Compton turned to face the smiling cook. "You wash your face and hands?" he asked impudently.

Charley Compton grinned boyishly. "Before I came into your kitchen, Woo," he answered. "Let's eat, Stingaree," he said to Burke. "We might have to ride out to give Gospel and the boss a hand!"

He dropped to his knees when a nose nudged his right knee. The black dog was asking for attention, and Compton put his arms around the sleek neck.

"That was mighty fine work, Major," he praised. "Remind me to save you my next steak bone."

"I'll sleep in the bunk house with you fellows," Burke told Compton. "We can talk better that way, and there are some things Mona Belle does not know."

"There are a lot of things I don't know," Compton answered, as he led the way to the big kitchen.

"Save it for later," Burke warned quietly. "The

world wasn't made in a day, and a part of this puzzle is nearly a hundred years old!"

## CHAPTER SIX

Ace Fleming watched Gospel Cummings as the gaunt plainsman followed a trail that would have been unseen by less trained eyes. They were deep in the badlands; had crossed a land-bridge where Lost River went underground. A steep trail cut through the dense brush leading to a sawed-tooth ridge, and Cummings called a halt as he turned his horse to face Yancey and Fleming.

"We might as well go back," he said wearily. "The man we are following is part of the Demingway gang, and he's in the cave by now. They could pick us off one at a time before we could even see their lookouts."

Ace Fleming rubbed the handles of his twin six-shooters. His little daughter was the pride of his life, and schooled as he was at hiding his emotions, his agitation was visible on his handsome face.

"We'll get back here at daylight," Cummings suggested quietly. "I might even be able to get into the cave through the chimney."

"Not any more, Gospel," Fleming argued. "Every one in the Strip knows about that secret entrance by now; you wouldn't have a chance!"

"Even I know about that way through the chimney," Skid Yancey added. "We'd better wait till daylight, boss. Besides, I have a hunch that Charley and Stingaree will have news for us."

"Quiet," Cummings said tensely. "Somebody coming up the back trail. Dismount and fan out; we'll jump whoever it is, and ask questions later!"

The faint sounds of a shod horse could be heard coming along the brushy trail from the east. Skid Yancey took down his catch-rope, tied up his horse, and crouched in the trailside brush. A horse loomed up in the dark, and Yancey made a bullet-cast with his noose.

Yancey hip-leaned against the rope as the startled horse shied to the left. A tall man was jerked from the saddle, and as he struck the ground, Ace Fleming leaped on the rider and struck once with his clubbed six-shooter. Gospel Cummings seized the dragging reins and quieted the spooky horse which he tied to a 'squite root before coming back to his companions.

"Do you know this hombre?" Fleming asked.

Cummings leaned closer and tried to find enough light for a possible identification. "I don't know him personal, but it's a gent by the name of Jack Barson," he stated. "He's one of Demingway's men, and he might have had something to do with the kidnapping. Hobble his hands and we will take him back to the Circle F."

Yancey took a piggin' string and tied the unconscious man's hands behind his back. They boosted Barson to the saddle of his own horse, mounted up, and started back through the brush-choked trails. Again it was Cummings who first heard an alien sound.

"I hear a dog talking," he said slowly. "Must be that Major dog the girl was going to put on the scent."

"Better let me ride ahead a spell," Yancey suggested. "I know Major, and he knows me. Okay, boss?"

"Ride on," Fleming agreed. "If they have hurt Deloise?"

"If they have, I'll side you from here to Hades!" Cummings declared in a husky voice.

Skid Yancey rode at a fast walk, pointing to the faint baying of the dog. Then he gave a high shrill whistle and cocked his head to listen. Silence for a moment, and then the dog's answer came back to him, down the wind. Two minutes later Major ran up to Yancey's horse. Yancey dismounted and petted the big black dog as he talked soothingly. He knew that Stingaree Burke would be with Major, and had as sensitive hearing as Gospel Cummings. When he heard the clop of hooves, Yancey called softly.

"Up the trail, Stingaree. Yancey talking!"

Stingaree Burke rode up the trail, closely followed by Charley Compton. Gospel Cummings and Ace Fleming arrived at the same time from the west, and their prisoner was just rousing around.

"Stand back, Stingaree," Yancey warned. "We caught us a prisoner, and look at Major going for him!"

The retriever had smelled the ground, raced up to Barson's horse, and was jumping at the stirrup. Burke took a leash and fastened it to the dog's collar. Charley Compton spoke hurriedly to Ace Fleming.

"We found Deloise, Boss. We brought her home, and she isn't hurt a bit!"

"Thank heaven," Fleming said gratefully.

"Amen," Gospel Cummings added reverently.

"Down, Major," Burke commanded the excited dog. He turned to Fleming. "This hombre was one of the pair who took the little girl. What is your pleasure, Fleming?"

"We will take him back to the Circle F until I decide," Fleming answered. "I can't think right now, and if you gents don't mind, I'll ride on ahead to see Deloise and Sandra."

"You do that, and we'll take it slow," Cummings seconded the suggestion. "And tell Woo Fong to heat up the grub."

"You say this owl-hooter's name is Barson?" Compton asked slowly.

"Wait till the boss comes up on you, Compton!" the prisoner growled savagely.

"You know him?" Cummings asked curiously.

"I've met him a time or two," Compton answered.

"Put a gun in my hand and tie me loose, is all I ask," Barson begged his captors. "That yearling gunhawk never saw the day he could match me with a six-shooter!"

"I matched you one time," Compton said coldly. "I should have killed you that time, but I threw off my shot!"

Barson swore hoarsely. "But you ain't a Texas Ranger no more!"

"Let's ride," Stingaree Burke said shortly. "If this whining snake wants to talk a lot, he can do it back on the Circle F. If he don't give up head and talk with a straight tongue, there's ways to persuade his kind!"

Charley Compton rode ahead with Burke, while Gospel Cummings paired with Yancey who was leading the prisoner's horse. They rode into the Circle F yard under the light of a young moon, and Yancey helped the prisoner dismount. As the party walked across the wide front porch, Ace Fleming opened the big door. He held Deloise in his arms, and she held out her arms to Cummings.

"You didn't come to see Sugar-Foots," the child complained.

Cummings took the little girl and held her very close for a long moment. His eyes were closed, and his lips seemed to be moving as though in silent prayer.

"I came when I could, little sweetheart," he told the child. "I have been very busy, but I love you almost twice as much as I did the last time."

He kissed the child on the cheek, and Deloise giggled. "Your whiskers tickle," she complained. "But I like it, Uncle Gospel."

Cummings handed the child to Sandra Fleming as Compton came into the room with Barson. The baby stared at Barson and started to tremble.

"He took me away!" she wailed. "He was with an ugly little man!"

"Did he hold his mouth like this?" Charley Compton asked, and he drew up his mouth as though it were pulled by a scar.

"Ooh, Charley, you look just like him," Deloise exclaimed. "His name was—"

"Cuchillo?" Compton prompted.

"Yes, Cuchillo," the little girl answered with a shudder.

"That means knife," Burke explained. "Cuchillo Lopez is a Mexican outlaw wanted on both sides of the border!"

"Better put Deloise to bed, Sandra," Ace Fleming told his pretty wife. "We want to have a talk with Barson. Please don't disturb us."

Ace Fleming walked up to the sullen prisoner. "Now you start talking, Barson," he said quietly. "And you tell it straight, or I'll work you over myself!"

Barson glanced down at the small gambler.

"You and who else?" he sneered.

Fleming stepped forward quickly. His hands flashed up and closed around the big outlaw's biceps. Then Fleming exerted his tremendous strength, and Jack Barson gasped and then screamed.

"Take him off, or tie me loose!"

Ace Fleming continued his pressure. His thumbs depressed the brachial points in the big man's arms, and Barson began to moan softly. "Talk!" Fleming said sternly. "Or you will never use your arms again!"

"Cord Demingway is after the treasure!" Barson gasped, as the sweat dripped from his face. "Swifty Matthews is after it, and so is Stingaree Burke!"

Fleming lessened the pressure a trifle. "What treasure?" he asked quietly.

"The Vallejo treasure!" Barson whimpered. "Leave me loose; my arms are killing me!"

Ace Fleming released his hold and stepped back. He watched the prisoner's face, and turned to Stingaree Burke.

"You want to say something, Burke?" he asked.

"It was just a gambler's chance, and I took it," Burke answered, tight-lipped. "I'm riding back to Dog Town to see Cuchillo Lopez!"

"I'll ride with you," Skid Yancey said eagerly. "I want to see Lilly Mae, and the hombre who sucked her into this deal!"

"You stay here, Skid," Fleming said quietly. "You'd just ride into a trap, and you're a sucker for the kind of bait Pug Jones uses!"

Fleming watched the face of Stingaree Burke as he spoke. Burke frowned and turned slowly. "Are you guessing?" he asked the little gambler.

"Ask Barson," Fleming suggested. "Perhaps he wants to talk some more, now that he can use his arms again."

"Pug will kill you for this, Burke," Barson said spitefully. "He's got a piece of that treasure!"

"Which piece?" Fleming asked. "Demingway or Matthews?"

Jack Barson raised his head with a startled gleam in his greenish eyes. "Say!" he ejaculated. "I never thought of that!"

"Did you think of it, Burke?" Fleming asked carelessly.

Stingaree Burke poured tobacco flakes in a brown-paper trough. His hands were steady, but his face was troubled.

"I hadn't thought of it, not after what happened to Tom Jenkins," he said thoughtfully. "Jenkins was one of Pug's men; he was killed by the Demingway crowd the morning we rode out to Lost River!"

"He was a dirty double-crosser," Barson said viciously. "Jenkins was one of Swifty Matthews' men!"

"Looks like Pug Jones is working both ends against

the middle," Fleming guessed shrewdly. He glanced
at Charley Compton, who was listening silently.

"Where do you fit into this puzzle, Charley?"
Fleming asked bluntly.

"Was a time I worked for Stingaree," Compton
answered without hesitation.

"You a lawman?" Fleming asked.

Stingaree Burke shook his white head. "I was raising cattle," he answered. "Charley was my foreman."

"I remember a brand called the Box V," Gospel
Cummings interrupted. "It was registered to the old
Vallejo Rancho down near Laredo."

"It still is," Burke said coldly.

"You eat now?" Woo asked from the doorway to
the kitchen. "Alla time talkee, talkee. Grub get plenty
cold. Come and get it!"

"I've eaten," Compton said shortly. "I'll keep a
gun on Barson while he stokes his innards."

"I'll watch Barson," Burke corrected. "Someone
wants to talk to you out on the porch. *Vamos!*"

Charley Compton stared and then hurried to the
front door. There was a swing in the shadows over
in a far corner of the long verandah, and Compton
walked slowly over when he heard the swing creak
slightly.

"Mona Belle?" he called in a whisper.

"Charley, please come and sit down."

Compton crossed the porch, trying to slow his

pace. He took a seat in the swing at the far end from the girl. He waited for her to speak.

"I heard what Barson said," the girl spoke in a subdued whisper. "What does it all mean, Charley?"

"I don't want to quarrel," Compton answered gruffly. "That's what came between us down in Texas." "But this is not Texas," Mona Belle said patiently. "Perhaps I was wrong, but I am also confused."

"You think you are confused?" Compton said bitterly.

"Please come closer; we might be overheard," the girl suggested.

Charley Compton grunted, but he moved close to the girl. "Please don't be angry," Mona Belle pleaded. "If I was wrong, I want to know, so I can correct any mistakes I made."

"You made one," Compton said savagely, "by trusting Swifty Matthews!"

"Mr. Matthews is a fine man," the girl defended him. "You and he used to be very good friends, when you were both Texas Rangers!"

"That was before he went bad and joined the Wild Bunch," Compton argued. "I got the word that he was gunning for me!"

"Is that why you followed him up here?" the girl asked.

"Partly; you know the rest of it!"

"The treasure," Mona Belle whispered softly. "I wonder if there really was a treasure?"

"There *was* one," Compton said gruffly. "Whether it still exists is the question."

"You were with Uncle Jose Morales when he died," the girl said slowly. "He would talk to no one but you. What did he tell you, Charley?"

"Just what he told you and Stingaree," Compton answered sullenly. "That there was a big treasure in gold bullion and jewels."

"But the title to the ranch is in question," Mona Belle said worriedly. "Uncle Burke was a lawyer; he knows about such things."

"Blast the treasure!" Compton burst out. "There's something else more valuable!"

"If I lose the ranch, I've lost everything," the girl said hopelessly.

"Everything?" Compton repeated.

"Everything except you and Uncle Burke, and the friendship of Malden Matthews," the girl said listlessly.

"I don't even like his name," Compton growled. "Swifty fits him better than Malden, the no-good owl-hooter!"

"You can't talk that way about my friends," Mona Belle answered heatedly. "You have no proof that he is an outlaw!"

"He's hip-deep with Pug Jones over at Dog Town,"

Compton argued. "And you know all about Jones!"

The girl shuddered. "Yes, I know all about Pug Jones," she admitted. "I'm afraid of Jones, and he does not like you since you argued with him."

"You won't go back there to sing any more," Compton stated positively.

"I might," Mona Belle said quickly. "If it would help Uncle Burke get any information."

"You stay away from there," Compton said roughly.

"Don't you give me orders, Charley Compton," the girl said angrily.

"I'm sorry," Compton said at once, and then he quickly seized the girl in his arms. "Don't do these things to me, Mona," he whispered huskily. "I love you too much, and I'd kill the man who hurt you!"

"Release me, Charley," Mona Belle said coldly. "I don't like to be man-handled by anyone!"

Charley Compton dropped his arms, and rose quickly to his feet. He left the startled girl and stomped across the porch with his spurs dragging. He almost bumped into Skid Yancey, who was leaving the front room.

"C'mon," Yancey said guardedly. "I'm riding to Dog Town, and I'd be proud to have you guard my back!"

"*Sta bueno,*" Compton agreed without hesitation. "I could work off a head of steam myself!"

They were saddling up when a voice spoke

inquiringly.

"You gents riding off some place?"

"Gospel!" Compton muttered. "What in time you doing back here in the dark?"

"Minding my own business," Cummings answered gruffly, but he wiped his silky brown beard with one lean hand. "You two heading for Dog Town?"

"Is that minding your own business?" Yancey demanded.

"Lay your hackles, cowboy," Cummings said sternly. "I was thinking some of riding yonderly myself."

"Surprise!" Yancey said acidly. "Call out the troops; we need a lot of help!"

"You get smart with me, I'll take you apart with my hands," Cummings threatened. "You'll need all the help you can get, and you both know it."

"You can't go," Yancey said nastily. "You've got to bend the lead to Lost River in the early morning."

"I'll be back before the early morning," Cummings said, and threw his saddle on a Circle F horse. "I might need your help then, so I'll help you now."

"Look, Gospel," Compton said soothingly. "You ain't as young as you used to be by at least twenty years. You need your sleep."

"A cowboy can make up his sleep come winter," Cummings remarked dryly, and went on saddling. "Who is it, Pug Jones or Cuchillo Lopez?"

"The old son is a mind-reader," Yancey remarked

to Compton. "I'm looking up this knife-throwing Mexican," he admitted grudgingly.

"Don't underrate Lopez," Compton warned. "He does not know the meaning of fear, and he can shoot mighty straight."

"He forced Lilly Mae to do what she did," Yancey argued. "I likewise want to see Lilly Mae!"

"Bull frog!" Cummings said dryly. "Lilly Mae is a gold-digger, and everyone knows it."

Charley Compton listened intently. It was not like Gospel Cummings to speak disparagingly of any woman; the old plainsman must have a good reason.

"How about you, Charley?" Cummings asked.

"What about me?"

"What's taking you back to Dog Town at this time of night?"

"Cuchillo Lopez," Compton answered without hesitation.

"Something to do with the Vallejo Rancho?" Cummings asked quietly.

"That's right."

"Mebbe we better take Ace along," Cummings suggested. "He's mixed up in this up to his hips, even if he does not understand all he knows about it!"

"How do you figure?" Yancey asked.

"Didn't they kidnap Sugar-Foots?" Cummings asked. "And Lost River Cave is on Circle F range."

"Just hold it a minute," a voice spoke from outside

the barn entrance. "Gospel is right, and I'll ride in with you. Now hold the talk till we quit the ranch; everyone is overhearing everyone else tonight."

Charley Compton felt his pulses quicken at Fleming's words. He wondered if he had been overheard talking with Mona Belle.

"Seems like we are all here except Stingaree Burke," he said lamely.

"How wrong can one gent be?" a voice asked sarcastically, and Burke entered the barn and took down his saddle. "I'd like a few words with Cuchillo Lopez myself!"

"What you reckon the boss and old Gospel have on their minds?" Yancey whispered with his mouth close to Compton's ear.

"Cuchillo Lopez," Compton answered dryly. "Let's go along for the ride."

"And perhaps earn your fighting pay," Ace Fleming said crisply. "If there is treasure on Circle F range, I want to know more about it. And I want to see this Lopez hombre the worst way!"

They left the Circle F at a quiet walk, remaining silent until they were well away from the big yard. Then Gospel Cummings spoke for his companions.

"What's your plan, Ace?"

"Thanks, Gospel," Fleming voiced his gratitude for the plainsman's understanding. "I want a talk with Pug Jones, and I figure Lopez will be there.

Now we know there is a connection between Pug Jones and Cord Demingway, and it also seems that Jones is stringing along with this Swifty Matthews. I'm using the excuse of my daughter's kidnapping, but I admit to you men that it is only an excuse. I'll settle for that personally when the time is right!"

"So we'll stop first at the Red Rose," Cummings said quietly. "Don't forget we were going to Lost River in the early morning."

"So we might have some information before we go there," Fleming answered harshly. "Those two kidnappers split up, and they went two ways. Perhaps Pug Jones can tell us why!"

Charley Compton nudged Skid Yancey gently. Both were under the domination of Ace Fleming's magnetism, and the gambler was making plans where they had intended to barge in looking for trouble just to work off their separate angers.

"You stay with the bunch, Skid," Fleming told Yancey. "Don't go bolting off alone to see about Lilly Mae!"

"Like you say, boss," Yancey answered.

"And you, Charley," Fleming continued sternly. "Leave Lopez to me!"

"I can take orders," Compton answered stiffly.

"They won't be expecting us tonight," Fleming said confidently. "Not after what happened tonight up at Lilly Mae's place. Yonder's the lights of Dog

Town, so let's ride in quietly."

They approached the saloon riding two abreast, with Ace Fleming in the lead. He stopped his horse abruptly, and the other four reined in quickly.

"Look there at the tie-rail," Fleming whispered. "That's Saint John's horse, and that big law-dog just might need some help!"

"The devil with him," Skid Yancey said bluntly. "That big jasper is all paw-and-beller, and he tells it scarey. Let him help himself!"

Suddenly men began to yell inside the saloon. The five riders dismounted and tied up at the rack. Then they were running toward the saloon where the bull-like voice of John Saint John was yelling for order.

"I'm the law here in the Strip!" the big deputy shouted. "I'm taking Lopez back to Vaca if I have to fight every gun-hung hombre in this sink of sin!"

"Hold it!" Fleming said quietly, and he stopped to peer under the slatted, swinging doors.

Saint John had his back to the door, and his gun covered a small Mexican with a twisted mouth. A big man stepped up behind Saint John and clubbed with his gun, and the deputy went down under the blow like a pole-axed steer.

Men swarmed toward the fallen man, and Ace Fleming slipped under the door with a six-shooter in each small hand.

"Stand away from the law!" the little gambler ordered sternly.

The doors opened silently, and Stingaree Burke stepped in, followed by Cummings, Compton, and Yancey.

## CHAPTER SEVEN

Ace Fleming faced the threatening crowd, backed up by his four seasoned companions. Percentage girls gaped from the sidelines. Tough gunmen stood frozen where the surprise had caught them, watching and waiting for an opportunity to earn their fighting pay. Fleming spoke softly to Cuchillo Lopez.

"You were to the Circle F this afternoon, *Señor* Lopez?"

Lopez gasped, and then straightened up. "Prove it!" he said brazenly. "I don't know you, *Señor!*"

"The name is Ace Fleming, father of the little girl you kidnapped. You, *Señor,* are a sneaking, cowardly dog!"

"Don't you come barging into my place with a cutter in each hand, and tell someone else they are a coward!" Pug Jones interrupted harshly.

Ace Fleming moved his smooth white hands. The two six-shooters disappeared in his holsters. He said quietly to Lopez, "You are the son of one she-dog!"

Cuchillo Lopez slapped for the knife he carried in

a sheath at the back of his neck. His hand came out of his shirt collar, clutching a balanced throwing knife. Ace Fleming struck for his right holster; pale flame winked out under the garish yellow lights of the hanging coal-oil lamps, as the long-barreled six-shooter exploded in the gambler's hand.

Lopez was jerked around to the right as the speeding slug hit his hand, and sent the knife spinning toward a side wall. Lopez stomped his boot to stop his turn. His left hand went down to his holster; his six-shooter was just clearing leather when Fleming squeezed off a slow shot. Lopez screamed with pain; he was like a vicious hawk with both wings broken and bleeding.

"Anyone else buying in?" Fleming asked softly. "How about you, Pug?"

"I never play the other man's game," Jones answered sullenly. "When I'm dealing, things will be different!"

"Do you know a gun-hand by the name of Jack Barson?" Fleming asked the saloon-man.

"I know him; works for Cord Demingway."

"We caught him," Fleming said sternly. "He was the other hombre who took my little girl. Barson talked with his mouth wide open; he told us a few things about you."

"Yeah; what you aim to do about it?" Jones asked slowly.

"You've seen me work one time," Fleming warned. "That's what I'll always do about it!"

Saint John moaned and rolled up to a sitting position. He shook his head to clear away the cobwebs of fog, and then he leaped to his feet.

"You're under arrest, Pug Jones!" he shouted. "For resisting arrest, and assaulting an officer!"

"Back up and take a fresh start, Saint," Fleming said quietly.

The deputy whirled and saw the five men from Vaca town. His jaw dropped with surprise, and then he rubbed a swelling on his shaggy head.

"What are you men doing here?" he demanded.

"Saving your life," Gospel Cummings said brusquely. "Yonder is your prisoner. He's one of the hombres who kidnapped Fleming's little girl!"

Saint John turned his attention to Pug Jones. "I'm warning you now, Jones," he said, and now his big voice was muted and low. "I mean to close you up and burn Dog Town to the ground. I'll do it the next time you get out of line!"

"Try it," Jones answered defiantly. "You make a pretty big target, and you won't live long after you strike the first match!"

"You men get out and mount up," Fleming took over to give orders. "Compton and I will stay here to cover this outfit until you ride up. Then you keep them covered while we get outside. And if any of you gents want to turn hero, we won't throw off our shots next time!"

"When you ride off, don't come back," Pug Jones warned viciously. "My men will shoot to kill the first one of you law-hounds that comes looking for trouble!"

Ace Fleming stiffened as he stared at the ugly twisted face of the Dog Town boss. "There ain't room enough here in the Strip for both of us, Jones," he said slowly, but his deep voice was vibrating with anger. "Thanks for the warning, and that goes both ways. We will also shoot on sight!"

Fleming and Compton backed out and mounted their horses. Then the party reined their horses and made a quick turn around a corner. They rode at a trot to an alley, with Burke leading the way. A low whistle came from Burke's little white house.

"Take it easy, Stingaree; Tim Kelly speaking."

Burke swung down and stepped into the shadows. "Howdy, Tim," he greeted the barkeep from the Silver Dollar. "You better ride out with us."

"Figured on doing it," Kelly answered with a chuckle. "I came over here and packed up most of the stuff belonging to you and Mona Belle. Got a pack mare out back, and we can carry the rest of the gear!"

After watching Kelly for a time, Skid Yancey spoke softly to Charley Compton.

"I never drank in the Silver Dollar, but if Kelly is a bardog, I'm a Mexican hairless. He rides like a cowboy, and he looks like the law to me!"

Charley Compton grunted; he had not spoken all during the fight in the Red Rose. The party reached the Circle F just before midnight, and it was Gospel Cummings who gave the orders for the coming day.

"We're hitting out for Lost River come daybreak, cowhands. It won't take long to spend the night here on the Circle F, so you better hit your soogans, and get what shut-eye you can."

Fleming said bluntly, "Saint, you better ride in with your prisoners, and get Lopez to the doctor."

Gospel Cummings sighed. "I'll ride down as far as Three Points with you," he told the deputy. "Just in case Demingway got word and figures on a rescue."

Charley Compton spoke hesitantly.

"I better ride along with Gospel," he suggested. "I can use that extra bunk in his cabin, and ride over here early for breakfast, if you say the word, boss."

"Thanks, Charley," Fleming said gratefully. "You fellows better be getting along. The rest of you turn in."

Gospel Cummings rode in moody silence, and Charley Compton had nothing to say. When they reached Three Points, Saint John's tone was conciliatory as he spoke to Compton.

"You were a lawman one time, Compton. Mind

riding into Vaca with me until I herd these hombres to the doctor's place?"

"Putting it that away, I can't refuse," Compton agreed grudgingly. "I'll be back as soon as I can, Gospel," he said to Cummings. . . .

"Rise and shine, cowboy," Cummings said gruffly. "I've got a pot of Arbuckle boiling to give us strength for the road."

"Like you said, Gospel," Compton complained. "It didn't take long to spend the night here."

Cummings had lighted the lamp, and a fire was going in the old iron stove. The fragrant aroma of coffee filled the little cabin as the two men washed in a granite basin. Cummings poured two huge mugs of steaming coffee, and Compton rolled a cigarette.

"Swifty Matthews," Cummings began abruptly. "One time he was a Texas Ranger, the same as you. How come he went wrong and joined up with the wild bunch?"

"It was his own idea," Compton answered reluctantly. "He and I were members of Company B at the same time. A braver man never drew breath, I'll give him that much. I reckon he wasn't making money fast enough."

"He don't look like an outlaw to me," Cummings said slowly.

Compton glanced up from his coffee. "You know him?"

"I've seen him," Cummings answered. "He still looks like a lawman to me. For that matter, so do you!"

"Nah uh," Compton said carelessly. "Saint John looks like a lawman. This is mighty good coffee."

The first fingers of dawn were showing against the eastern sky as the two men entered the little barn. Charley Compton stopped suddenly. He stared at his saddle which was hanging from a peg near the door. Cummings followed his gaze and spoke worriedly.

"We had visitors while we slept. What was you carrying under your saddle-skirts?"

Compton stepped up to his saddle and fingered the leather. Some one had used a sharp knife to cut the stitching, and Compton swore under his breath.

"It was a map," he told Cummings.

"To the Vallejo treasure?" Cummings asked.

Compton nodded his head. "I got it from old Jose Morales who was kin to Don Alvarado Vallejo," he explained. "He gave it to me just before he died, and that's what brought me up here to the Strip! It won't do Cord Demingway much good. I changed it some; I've got the real map in my head."

They saddled their horses and rode up the trail in the very early dawn. Just before they reached the

Circle F, Compton spoke quietly.

"I'd rather you didn't say anything about the map, Gospel."

"Like you say, Charley."

Shorty Benson met them at the Circle F barn and said he would change their gear to fresh horses. They hurried to the big kitchen where the rest of the men were just finishing breakfast. Woo Fong had two places ready, and Compton and Cummings started their breakfast.

"Every man packs a rifle today," Fleming said gruffly. "What's this about Demingway panning gold on Circle F range?" And he stared at Gospel Cummings.

"There always has been a trace of metal back there near Lost River," Cummings said carelessly. "You knew it, Ace."

"Not enough for a getaway stake to South America," the Circle F owner said flatly. "Why didn't you tell me, Gospel?"

Cummings finished his breakfast and wiped his silky beard with his left hand. "I thought Vaca would be well rid of Demingway if that was all he wanted," he answered. "I thought it just might keep down a few killings."

"We've never pampered outlaws before up here in the Strip," Fleming said a trifle sharply. "They've tried to rustle our cattle several times, and most of them are now in Boot Hill."

"We haven't done so bad this time, boss," Skid Yancey said proudly.

"There are conflicting forces opposed to each other up here," Fleming said thoughtfully. "Not one or two, but half a dozen or more!"

He glanced briefly at the face of Stingaree Burke, went on to Charley Compton, and stopped at Tim Kelly. The three men remained silent, and Fleming appealed to Gospel Cummings.

"Out with it, old sign-reader," he said bluntly. "What's the score the way you see it?"

Gospel Cummings stroked his full brown beard. He shook his head slowly, and there was a slight tremble in his hand.

"I'm puzzled too, Ace," he admitted honestly. "We've got a jigsaw puzzle here, and the pieces are scattered all over the place. Like every other puzzle, here and there we find a small piece which seems to fit in with what we already have. For instance, where does Swifty Matthews fit into the picture?"

Compton raised his head and stared at Cummings. Stingaree Burke was also watching the tall plainsman; there was the trace of a smile on the tall bartender's smooth face.

"Charley knows Matthews better than we do," Cummings said slowly. "They were in the Texas Rangers together at one time."

Fleming glanced at Compton. "So?" he asked.

"I'd rather not say what I don't know for sure," Compton answered honestly. "When I was riding the long trails, there was no man I'd rather have side me than Swifty Matthews."

"You mean the *law* trails," Fleming said clearly.

"That's right."

"He's likewise a friend of Mona Belle," Fleming said quietly. "Burke is her uncle, and one time he worked for Burke."

"Best cow foreman I ever saw," Stingaree Burke praised him warmly. "If there is such a thing as the old Vallejo treasure, the Box V needs it."

"Cuchillo Lopez," Fleming said slowly. "Jack Barson. They both knew about the Vallejo treasure. They belonged to the Demingway gang."

"So the pieces are fitting together some," Cummings said with a smile. "We better get started for Lost River, and see if we can find any more of those missing pieces."

Gospel Cummings spoke briefly.

"Seven of us," he commented. "I'll ride with Burke and Compton. Yancey and Kelly ride with Ace Fleming. Shorty Benson will ride as rear guard and see to the horses if we have to go part of the way on foot. Let's head back for the lavas."

The men nodded. Someone had to give orders, and Gospel Cummings was eminently qualified. He knew the badlands better than any of them; it was he who had first discovered the secret entrance to Lost River Cave. No longer a secret, but it would provide a second entrance into the stronghold of the outlaws.

Charley Compton glanced at his torn saddle-skirt, and then stared at Shorty Benson. Benson smiled; he had stitched up the rent in the leather while Compton and Cummings had eaten breakfast.

An hour and six miles later, they came to the brawling stream known as Lost River. Gospel Cummings called a halt and cupped his old field glasses to his eyes. He gasped when he focused on a certain spot high above the trail, well out of rifle range. Another man was watching him through a pair of field glasses. As he watched, the man lowered his glasses and thumbed his nose with his left hand.

"Pride goeth before a fall, and a haughty spirit before destruction," Cummings said gravely. "The stiff neck shall be bowed!"

"What the devil's he talking about?" Tim Kelly asked Fleming.

"Gospel saw something," Fleming said positively. "What is it, Gospel?"

"There's an hombre about a mile from here on a high ledge," Cummings explained. "When I put my glasses on him, he was staring at me through a pair of his own. He thumbed his nose at me!"

Yancey chuckled. "Who is this jasper?"

"The head man," Cummings said quietly. "It was Cord Demingway, but now he's gone."

"Preparing a reception committee for us," Fleming said quietly. "You got any plans?"

"It's either war or a parley," Cummings said thoughtfully. "Do I hear any suggestions?"

Ace Fleming frowned. "War would mean a long-distance sniping affair," he said slowly. "Do you reckon they'd talk?"

Gospel Cummings straightened slowly. "I wonder if Demingway savvies the sign language?" he asked. "If he does, he could put his glasses on me, and I could talk some with my hands."

He cupped the glasses to his eyes, stared intently, and then began to make motions with the long fingers of his right hand. When he stopped, he again stared intently through his glasses. Then he sighed with disappointment.

"What did he say?" Burke asked.

"He said to go to the devil," Cummings answered. "Said to tell Stingaree Burke he had what he wanted!"

"He must mean the old map," Burke muttered, and then he trapped his thin lips tight.

"What map?" Fleming asked.

"An old Mexican map giving the location of the Vallejo treasure," Burke answered reluctantly. "We never did find it, although there are several inaccurate copies."

Shorty Benson listened and stared at Compton's saddle.

"Ask Charley," he said quietly. "He was robbed last night while he was asleep."

Compton whipped about in the saddle and glared angrily at the short-legged cowboy. Now another piece of the puzzle had been found—or lost.

Ace Fleming said sternly, "Did you lose a map, Compton?"

Compton glanced at Stingaree Burke. Then he slowly nodded his head. "I had one sewed up between my saddle-skirts," he admitted.

"You fool!" Burke burst out. "That's the first place an outlaw would look. That's the place where every one of them carry posters of themselves. You know that as well as I do!"

"I reckon I do."

"Where did you get the map?" Burke demanded.

"From old Jose Morales the night he died," Compton answered hopelessly. "He told me to memorize it in my head, and then destroy it."

"So you had to sew it in the skirts of your saddle!" Burke said scathingly. "And you never told me or Mona Belle anything about it!"

"I made a promise to Jose," Compton murmured.

"This map," Burke asked caustically. "It gave the location of the treasure?"

Compton nodded moodily.

"Where was it?" Burke demanded.

"In Lost River Cave!"

"Charley, I ought to kill you!" Burke burst out as his temper slipped completely. "We needed that treasure to re-stock the ranch, after and providing we can prove ownership to the land-grant!"

"Make sign-talk to Demingway," Fleming said to Cummings. "Tell him they have forty-eight hours to clear out of the Strip, or we will plant them right here!"

Cummings raised his glasses. Then the fingers of his right hand began to move in the sign language.

"What did he say?" Fleming asked, as Cummings lowered his glasses.

"The same as before," Cummings answered.

"We could block all means of escape to the out-side," Charley Compton suggested. "On top of that, they won't find the treasure in forty-eight hours!"

Every man in the group stared at him. Compton smiled for the first time, and he winked at old Sting-aree Burke. Burke stared and blew through his lips. Then he shook his head.

"I don't get it, but I've never known you to go off half-cocked up to now," he said worriedly.

"Mebbe Swifty Matthews will bring fight to Dem-ingway," Skid Yancey said hopefully.

"Mebbe he will," Compton replied. "I hope so."

"I knew it," Gospel Cummings said with a grimace. "Here comes the law. Let me warn all you hombres in advance. Saint John will try to swear us all in as a posse. You gents can suit yourself, but I'm going back home to Three Points!"

## CHAPTER EIGHT

John Saint John galloped his big gray gelding when he saw the group of men preparing to quit the badlands. The big deputy blocked the narrow trail effectively by the simple expedient of broad-siding his horse across it.

"There's been murder done, boys!" he shouted. "I deputize you all as a special posse to ride in after the killer!"

"Killers," Compton corrected dryly. "There's more than one of them."

"How did you know?" Saint John demanded in surprise.

"It figured," Compton answered promptly. "When you went to the jail this morning, you found Cuchillo Lopez and that big gun-hawk both dead. He talked plenty before you took him to Vaca town," Compton added carelessly. "That's why I knew you'd wake up and find him dead some morning."

Gospel Cummings relaxed with a sigh of relief.

He was learning to respect Charley Compton's uncanny ability to foretell the actions and reactions of other men.

"They were shot through the window from the outside," Saint John offered weakly. "Lopez got it between the eyes, but that big hombre took two slugs between the shoulders. The sign left by two horses led this way; I knew the killers were part of the Demingway gang."

"Saved the law a lot of expense," Stingaree Burke muttered. "Like Fleming said, it makes our job easier, the more those owlhooters fight among themselves."

"We might as well get back to the Circle F and do the work we get paid to do," Skid Yancey suggested.

Saint John grudgingly yielded the trail. He rode back with the party to the forks where the Circle F men turned east. Gospel Cummings rode on toward Three Points, and the deputy hesitated and then rode with him.

"Being the law, I ought to tell you," Cummings said slowly. "After Charley rode back from Vaca last night, he stripped his riding gear and hung it in the barn. We slept three hours, but we had visitors from Lost River while we slept. Compton had an old map sewed between his saddle-skirts. It was gone when we went out to saddle up for the ride to the Circle F!"

"Why didn't you tell me back there?" the deputy demanded.

Cummings shrugged wearily. "We'd just been through it all with Charley," he explained. "You'd have sat tall in the saddle and gone through the whole go-around again, and tempers were touchy. Nothing you could do about it nohow. When are the funerals?"

"Tomorrow morning," Saint John accepted the change of subjects. "County jobs without fee to you."

Cummings nodded and rode back to his little barn. Saint John continued up the trail to Vaca, and after stripping his gear, Cummings walked slowly to his cabin and entered the open door. He smiled when he saw four gold pieces lying on his deal table; what Saint John didn't know would not bother his conscience.

Cummings pocketed the money and sat down to wait for the coffee to get hot. He opened the Book, started to read, and then raised his head slightly. He had heard no sound, but some sixth sense warned him of an alien presence. His right hand started to move slowly toward his holstered six-shooter.

"Let it ride, old-timer. I come in peace."

Cummings stopped his hand when a low deep voice spoke quietly. He did not turn, but his mind was busy checking voices he had heard. For a long moment he sat thus, and then he smiled.

"Come in, Matthews; enter under the sign of peace!"

A tall man stepped inside with his right hand held shoulder-high, the palm turned outward. Gospel Cummings made the same sign; motioned to a chair at the table.

"How did you know me?" Matthews asked curiously.

"I've never heard your voice before, but I recognized a note of youth and authority," Cummings explained. "I've talked quite a bit to Charley Compton. What's on your mind?"

"Charley Compton," Matthews answered without hesitation, thereby increasing the respect Cummings already had for him. "Charley and I used to be saddle pards and good friends. I wish it was that way again."

"The eternal triangle," Cummings murmured.

"I beg your pardon?"

"You don't," Cummings contradicted. "You know what I'm talking about, and facts are facts!"

"I reckon you are right, old-timer," Matthews admitted. "How much do you know?"

"Hmm," Cummings said musingly. "About what, for instance?"

"About Charley, Stingaree Burke, and Mona Belle," Matthews said more explicitly.

"Taking them in order, Charley was a Texas Ranger one time, and so were you," Cummings answered. "Burke was a lawyer, and manager of the Box V Ranch. Mona Belle was the owner of the

Vallejo Rancho carrying that brand. Now let me ask a question, and use your own judgment. What put you on the owl-hoot trail?"

Swifty Matthews glanced at Cummings, studied the lined face briefly, and quickly nodded. Matthews was an even six feet, fast in all his movements, but with a restraint unusual in one of his years.

"I'm a year older than Charley," he answered quietly. "Twenty-five to be exact. I was orphaned when I was ten; a man by the name of Joe Compton took me in and gave me a home. Yeah; Charley's father. He was sheriff of Webb County; Laredo was the county seat. That tell you anything, you being a Texas man your ownself?"

"Laredo is on the Rio Grande, right across from Mexico," Cummings said musingly, and then his brown eyes brightened. "The Vallejo Rancho is near Laredo," he continued. "Cord Demingway's brother was killed in Laredo by a gent name of Swifty Matthews. That adds quite a few pieces to the puzzle when put in their proper places."

Matthews frowned to show that he did not understand. "Puzzle?" he repeated.

"This whole matter of all you Texas folks coming up here in the Strip, Territory of Arizona," Cummings went on. "The Vallejo Rancho is in Webb County, Texas. The Vallejo treasure is supposed to be buried up here in the Strip. Now where does Pug

Jones fit in?"

"He's a killer," Matthews said quietly. "He had delusions of power. He's the boss of Dog Town like you know, but it goes much further than that."

"Mona Belle Courtney," Cummings said gently. "A beautiful girl with spirit."

"That's bait," Matthews said harshly. "I'm not taking it!"

"I didn't look you up," Cummings reminded. "You came here to see me. Why?"

"Because Mona Belle is in danger," Matthews answered sullenly.

"She has plenty of friends and protection now," Cummings answered. "She is staying at the Circle F with her uncle, and Charley Compton works for Ace Fleming. You were saying?"

"I've got to see her," Matthews said earnestly. "And I can't go to the Circle F!"

"Nuh uh," Cummings said sternly. "No you don't, Swifty Matthews. I won't be a go-between, and beside, Charley Compton is a friend of mine!"

"The stubborn knot-head!" Matthews said angrily. "He is a friend of mine too, or at least he used to be!"

"And he's in love with Mona Belle," Cummings said slowly. "So are you!"

Swifty Matthews jerked and laid his right hand on his holstered gun. Gospel Cummings moved with deceptive speed. His six-shooter leaped out and covered Matthews, who stared at the gaping muzzle and slowly raised his hands to a level with his ears.

"I'm sorry, Gospel Cummings," Matthews made his manners. "I should have known better after hearing about you. Yes, I'm in love with Mona Belle; I've always loved her!"

"So don't ask me to play Cupid," Cummings warned sternly. "You want to talk some more?"

"There's a document with that treasure," Matthews said slowly. "The original grant from the Mexican government; it's more than a hundred years old. Mona Belle is the only living relative of old Don Alvarado Vallejo. That grant would prove her ownership to the vast Vallejo Rancho!"

"Does Charley Compton know this?" Cummings asked.

"I couldn't say, but in some way we've got to find that treasure before Demingway or Pug Jones gets to it. The original grant was for two hundred thousand acres, but several small pieces have been sold down through the years."

"What's your own interest?" Cummings asked shrewdly.

"I own ten sections, about sixty-five hundred acres," Matthews answered honestly. "I don't mind admitting I won it in a poker game—from Joe Demingway."

"Just before you killed him?" Cummings asked.

"A week before," Matthews explained. "He asked for revenge, and tried to deal an ace off the bottom. He went for his gun, but he shot second. That's what put me to sleeping with the owls! There's no charge against me up here," Matthews said coldly. "Down in Texas, the witnesses were all friends of the deceased!"

"Where does Charley fit in?"

"That triangle you mentioned," Matthews said grimly. "On top of that, Charley owns, or he did own, twenty sections of the old grant. His father, Sheriff Joe Compton, bought it cheap during a long drought. It's all he left Charley, but right now a Syndicate claims ownership to the whole grant!"

"That's where Stingaree Burke fits in," Cummings murmured. "He's a law-sharp."

"There must have been a treasure map," Cummings said slowly.

"There are a dozen," Matthews agreed. "But there was only one authentic map, and Jose Morales had it. If the outlaws get that map, the Syndicate will win!"

"It does not seem to worry Charley Compton much," Cummings said with a shrug.

Matthews gasped and leaned forward. "What do you mean by that?" he asked sharply.

"The map was stolen from Charley last night," Cummings answered calmly. "He had it sewed be-

tween the skirts of his saddle, and one of Demingway's men must have found it last night while we
were asleep."

"I've got to see Charley!" Matthews said harshly.
"There is no reason why he and I can't work together!"

Cummings stroked his long brown beard. "I can
tell him what you said," he said thoughtfully. "Charley has nothing but praise for you, up to a certain
point. Those reasons are perhaps personal, and between you and him."

"Charley Compton does not know the meaning of
fear," Matthews said earnestly. "He don't go barging
in without first using his head. He was one of the best
rangers on the force, and I ought to know!"

"Yeah, that's right," Cummings agreed. "And he's
mighty fast with a six-shooter!"

He watched Matthews' face as he spoke. He was
surprised when Matthews nodded agreement.

"I'll be riding," Matthews made his decision
quickly. "If you see Charley, tell him what I said."

He went to the door, glanced down the road to
Vaca, and drew back. Then he glanced up at the
upper trail, and muttered something Cummings
could not understand.

"Any place I can hide?" Matthews asked anxiously.
"Charley is coming down the trail, and Saint John
riding in from Vaca."

"Behind that curtain where I keep my clothes," Cummings said gruffly. "That's the only place, and you are likely to be seen or heard."

Matthews slid behind the muslin curtain as a horse stopped at the tie-rail. A moment later Charley Compton rode down and dismounted, and both men came toward the cabin. Saint John came in first.

"Swifty Matthews was seen in the neighborhood. Have you seen him, Gospel?"

Cummings could see Charley Compton right behind the deputy, standing on the steps. "I was just fixing to grab a little sleep," Cummings complained.

"There's no rest for the wicked," Saint John said with a grin. "You didn't answer my question."

"I saw him," Cummings answered gruffly. "I see all kinds of people down here at the crossroads. Is that against the law?"

"When was he here?" Compton interrupted, as he edged in beside the deputy.

"This morning, not long since," Cummings replied.

"He's wanted for a killing down in Texas," Saint John stated. "I'd like to ask that gent a few questions."

"You've got no warrant for Matthews," Compton interrupted.

"Don't need one," Saint John said bluntly. "But he knows something about Demingway and that treasure everyone seems to be hunting, and treasure always leads to sudden death for somebody."

Charley Compton stomped out and mounted his horse. He started up the trail, watched until Saint John had ridden toward town, and then circled the little barn. He dismounted, ground-tied his horse with trailing whangs, and walked slowly back to the cabin. Gospel Cummings showed surprise when Compton came in.

"You forget something?" he asked.

Compton looked at the gaunt plainsman for a long moment. "I came back to have a talk with Swifty," he said quietly. "You're not a convincing liar, Gospel," he continued. "I saw that curtain move, and I saw a boot pulled back. Come on out—Malden!"

Swifty Matthews flipped the curtain and stepped into the room. His right hand was raised with the palm turned out in the sign of peace.

"How, Charley," he greeted Compton. "Long time no see."

"Howdy," Compton grunted. "You fool, why did you ride down here in broad daylight?"

"To have a talk with you," Matthews answered quickly. "Did you know that Pug Jones has about a dozen gun-fighters on his payroll?"

Compton showed that he did not understand. "I knew he had some," he admitted. "What's this got to do with me?"

"Mebbe nothing; perhaps everything," Matthews said with a shrug. "Pug Jones has a big piece of the Syndicate that is claiming the Vallejo Rancho. Most of them are from Texas, and they will head back there after this treasure hunt is over!"

"The devil you say!" Compton said jerkily, and then he eyed Matthews suspiciously. "How did you find out about the Syndicate?"

"Come off it, Charley," Matthews answered testily. "I found out about it the day after I won that ten sections of land from Joe Demingway, down in Laredo. I had to take to the brush after Demingway and I settled our differences, and I've kept my ear to the ground!"

"You called him Malden," Cummings said curiously.

"That's his name—his front handle," Compton said maliciously.

"Fiddle-faddle and chit-chat," Matthews said gruffly. "What's this I hear about you having the old map to the treasure, and losing it like a dude pilgrim?"

"You didn't hear that with an ear to the ground," Compton said angrily, and he turned on Gospel Cummings. "Well?" he said.

"Yeah, I told him," Cummings admitted. "Everyone else knows it, and I didn't think it was a secret any longer."

"It means war now," Matthews said quietly. "Just as soon as Pug Jones gets the news, he will attack Demingway with his full force!"

"Anything wrong with that?" Compton asked, and he gazed levelly at his one-time friend.

Swifty Matthews swallowed hard. "You mean to stand there and say you figured it like this?" he demanded. "When you know what that treasure means to Mona Belle?"

"That ten sections you won at poker used to belong to the Vallejo Rancho," Compton said coldly.

"So did the twenty sections you own!" Matthews retorted.

Charley Compton sighed and dropped his eyes. "Stalemate," Gospel Cummings said judiciously. "Why don't both you boys back off and try it again?"

"Cuchillo Lopez was a Demingway man," Matthews said suddenly. "Pug Jones knew it; that's why he made no real play to protect the Mexican."

"We haven't done bad up to now," Compton said slowly. "Tally the score, and you'll find all those hombres have been owl-hooters. The ones Gospel has sleeping back there in Hell's Half Acre," he added.

After a moment Cummings spoke in a quiet, gentle voice.

"You boys will have to fight together." And his words were like a prophecy. "The triangle can wait until later!"

Neither Matthews or Compton made any attempt to misunderstand. They stared into each other's eyes, faces hard, emotions running high. Swifty Matthews made the first overture.

"Here's my hand, Charley."

"The same to you, you blasted owl-hooter," Charley Compton answered in a savage growl, and his hand met the hard flesh of Matthews and gripped down like a vise.

"I wanted to warn you, Charley," Matthews said in a hard, brittle voice. "Pug Jones put a five thousand dollar reward on your scalp."

"Watch your back, Charley, or get Skid Yancey to do it."

"I wish it was you rubbing stirrups with me," Compton said, a trifle wistfully. *"Hasta la vista!"*

"Till we meet again," Matthews repeated, and he left the cabin and headed for a dim trail up behind the old barn.

"There rides a man, Charley," Cummings said at Compton's shoulder. "Which you might remember when the pay-off comes."

"Meaning?"

"You know what I mean," Cummings answered testily. "Right now you're setting a couple of traps to have those two outfits of owl-hooters take it to each other. You planted that map where you knew it would be found. I don't know what you have in mind beyond that point, but I can read the sign that far!"

"I better be riding back to the Circle F," Compton said abruptly. "I want to have a talk with somebody."

"Better make it old Stingaree," Cummings suggested. "He thinks a heap of you!"

## CHAPTER NINE

Mona Belle Courtney was waiting with Sandra Fleming on the large porch of the Circle F ranchhouse when Charley Compton rode into the yard. Mona Belle held little Deloise on her lap, and the child called to Compton who was riding on to the big barn.

"Come see me, Cholly. You come on up here!"

"Why, Howdy, Sugar-Foots," he greeted the child. "I had quite a talk with Malden," he added, looking at the lovely Mona.

"You must have work to do," Mona Belle said coldly. "I will go in and help Sandra."

"You are not interested in what Malden said?" Compton asked maliciously.

Sandra Fleming looked puzzled, but she took Deloise into the house, leaving Mona Belle and

Compton alone. Compton smiled wistfully and then glanced at the door.

"Want to take a walk over by the corral?" he asked.

Mona Belle arose reluctantly. Compton fell in beside her, picked up his trailing bridle-reins, and led his horse over to a large holding corral.

"We were overheard the last time we talked on the porch," Compton said just above his breath.

Mona Belle faced him squarely. "You had a map, and you didn't tell me," the girl accused him bitterly. "You got it from Jose Morales the night he died, but you kept it a secret."

"That's right," Compton agreed. "I had good reasons."

"Now the outlaws have the map," the girl continued angrily.

"Yeah," Compton admitted moodily.

"Did it give the exact location of the treasure?" Mona Belle asked.

"I'm afraid it did," Compton admitted reluctantly. "The treasure is hidden back there in Lost River Cave."

There was a strained silence for a long moment, and then the girl spoke. "What did Swifty have to say, and where did you see him?"

"Down at Gospel Cummings' cabin," Compton answered. "Malden was hiding behind a curtain, and

Saint John was there. He didn't see Malden," he added.

"Are you trying to irritate me?" the girl asked. "You always called him Swifty."

"Look, Mona Belle," Compton ground out savagely. "You have been irritating me for more than four months. There was a time when I thought we were more than just good friends, and now we don't seem even to be good friends."

"Was it friendly to withhold information from me?" the girl asked quietly. "After all, I am the great-granddaughter of Don Alvarado Vallejo, and his sole living relative."

"And heir," Compton added. "You own nearly all of the old land grant given to Don Alvarado, and which made up the Vallejo Rancho."

"Except for two pieces which my father sold," Mona Belle reminded. "Now you own twenty sections of the land."

"Malden owns the other ten sections," Compton said spitefully.

The girl drew back in startled surprise. "He does? I never knew about that!"

"It isn't a secret," Compton said bluntly. "That's the real reason Swifty is on the dodge," he added honestly. "He won it in a poker game from Joe Demingway back in Laredo. A week later Demingway tried to win back the land. He dealt an ace from the bottom of the deck, and then made a pass for his gun. Swifty was too fast for him, and they buried Joe Demingway. He wanted you to know!"

"Thank you for telling me, Charley," the girl said, and now her face was once more lovely when she smiled. "Swifty will sell that land back to me if we get this all straightened out." She stopped and glanced at his tanned face expectantly. "Well?" she asked.

"Yes," Compton said with a nod. "There's a deep well on my twenty sections."

"I know it," the girl said impatiently. "Your father had that well drilled, and I watched them bring it in."

"So did I," Compton growled.

"You will sell it to me?"

"No," Compton answered firmly. "I always figured to get the start of a spread down there. I still do!"

"Is this blackmail?" Mona Belle demanded.

"Sometimes a fella will give away what he won't sell," Compton said with a smile. "We can talk about that later, after this other business has been settled."

"If we clear up the title to the ranch, you will always have your old job as foreman of Rancho Vallejo," Mona Belle reminded him.

"Thanks, boss," Compton said coldly. "But with that twenty sections, I can always go there if I get fired."

"I almost hate you," Mona Belle said angrily. "When I tell Uncle Burke what you have said, he will know what to do!"

"You do that," Compton agreed. "I've already talked to Stingaree."

There was another long pause, and then Mona Belle came closer to Compton. "What else did Swifty say?" she asked hopefully.

"Now listen good," Compton said heavily, and he did not meet her dark eyes. "Pug Jones is in this thing up to his neck. He's repping for a Syndicate which is trying to get Rancho Vallejo. There is big money behind this Syndicate, and they want no part of Cord Demingway."

"That means Pug Jones and his hired gun-hands will make war on Demingway," Mona Belle said slowly. She looked closely at Compton. "Where does that leave you—and Swifty?" she asked.

"Swifty Matthews and I always fought together in the old days," Compton said sullenly. "There isn't any real reason why we should change now!"

Mona Belle stared at him and then gripped his arms. "You and Swifty would do this for me, Charley?" she whispered. "I like you both very much!"

She left him and returned to the big house. Charley Compton tied his horse and went to the bunkhouse. Stingaree Burke was looking over some papers he had taken from a bulging pair of saddle-bags. He glanced up at Compton inquiringly.

"Can you draw up a will?" Compton asked abruptly.

"I can," Burke answered. "Something important on your mind?"

"It could be," Compton said carelessly. "Make it simple and to the point. If anything happens to me, I want Mona Belle to have that twenty sections of land I own. You know all about it, the boundary descriptions, metes and bounds. Better do it as soon as you can."

Stingaree Burke studied the fighting face for a brief moment. "I'll have it done by supper time," he answered. "I'll be one witness; Ace Fleming all right with you for the other one?"

"Suits me fine, and Ace won't talk," Compton agreed.

"Be doubly careful from now on," Burke warned. "I heard about that bounty Pug Jones offered for the Syndicate!"

Compton seemed surprised. "How did you hear?" he asked.

"Tim Kelly has a friend in the Silver Dollar," Burke explained. "Tim took the night shift in the Casino to let Fat Farrell have a day off. This friend of Tim's rode over from Dog Town last night. You ever hear of an hombre named Brett Slagle?"

Charley Compton's nostrils began to flare. He nodded his head, and his right hand went to his six-shooter.

"I know the gent," he answered. "One of the fastest gun-hawks along the border. We played a game of draw one time; it ended that way. Why do you ask?"

"He's over at Dog Town," Burke answered slowly. "He's looking for you. Told it scarey that you and him had some unfinished business. Now I know what that business is!

"Tim said to warn you," Burke continued. "Slagle packs a hide-out gun under his left arm. Better stay away from Vaca for a while."

Compton stared at the white-haired lawyer. "Are you telling me to ride into Vaca?" he asked quietly.

"No," Burke said slowly. "But I knew you would. I wish you had Swifty Matthews to side you."

"I saw Swifty this morning," Compton said with a smile. "He was down at Three Points in Gospel's cabin. Mebbe you knew that too."

"The devil you whisper!" Burke ejaculated. "What did he want?"

"For one thing, he warned me about the bounty on my scalp," Compton answered. "The rest of it was personal."

Compton nodded and left the bunk-house. He rode up to the little office at one end of the big house. It wasn't a long walk, but horses were made to ride. Compton dismounted and entered the office.

"Good morning, boss," he began.

"I said good morning to you before sun-up," Fleming reminded him, and then he smiled. "Anything new?"

"Nothing you don't know," Compton replied. "You've heard about Brett Slagle and the Syndicate!"

"Yes," Fleming admitted. "What was your idea in planting that map where you knew it would be found?" he demanded suddenly.

Compton stared with his lips parted. "Who told you that?" he asked.

"Look, Charley," Fleming said bluntly. "I've been a gambler all my life. I've been a cattleman most of it too. I can read sign, and sometimes I can read men. Did you find any more pieces to the puzzle?"

Compton nodded. "I saw Swifty Matthews down at Three Points," he admitted.

"Yeah, I knew," Fleming said quietly.

"You knew? Who told you?"

"Saint John; he knew Matthews was behind that curtain at Gospel's!"

"I'll be hanged!" Compton said jerkily. "I didn't think that big moose saw Swifty's boot!"

"For one time the Saint used his head," Fleming said quietly. "He also knew he wouldn't get far with both you and Gospel."

"What did you want with me?" Compton asked lamely.

"I'm in the middle here," Fleming said slowly. "The treasure is near my land, and that gold mine is on Circle F range. You are working for me, and I'm losing beef. Now if you were me, what would you do?"

"I'd play both ends against the middle the same way you are doing it," Compton answered promptly. "Then I'd let human nature take its course, and stand by to give it a hand where needed."

Fleming smiled. "Look at how the cards lie," he continued. "Mona Belle and Stingaree Burke staying here at the Circle F. Tim Kelly working relief at the Casino. You on my payroll at fighting pay. Then there is Swifty Matthews, Brett Slagle, Pug Jones and Cord Demingway. That's quite a lay-out in any man's language."

"And it all ties in together," Compton added. "You're the boss!"

"I'm not sure about that," Fleming said doubtfully. "But we have fought outlaws up here before. Not only that, but each time Lost River Cave figured in the deal."

"Brett Slagle," Compton changed the subject, and now his voice was grim. "I'll have to give him a chance."

"Looks like," Fleming agreed at once. "Or you will be shot from the brush by a bushwhacker in the pay of Pug Jones. He will be at the Casino tonight, and I don't mind telling you that Slagle has all our men bluffed in Vaca."

"I don't like it that way," Compton demurred. "We've brought enough trouble to Vaca town, but we wouldn't have a chance taking it over to Dog Town."

"You've got this thing figured, Charley," Fleming accused bluntly. "After Slagle, then what?"

Charley Compton looked at Fleming for a long moment. He glanced around to see if they could be overheard.

"Demingway is trying to find the Vallejo treasure right now," Compton said confidently. "The Syndicate, and that means the outfit Jones is fronting for, wants the land grant more than anything else. They will move in against Cord Demingway and his gang. Now, what about the law, and I mean John Saint John?"

"Is there any other law up here?" Fleming asked quickly.

"I haven't been here long," Compton countered. "Is there?"

"I believe there is, but pass that for now," Fleming answered with a smile. "The Saint has a nose for trouble, and he usually shows up sooner or later. I happen to know that he is riding out here tonight to make talk with Stingaree Burke."

"So what do you want Skid Yancey and me to do tonight?" Compton asked innocently.

Ace Fleming had been a gambler all his life; he thoroughly enjoyed a battle of wits. He watched Compton's fighting face and liked what he saw.

"Tim Kelly will be helping Fat Farrel at the Casino tonight," he said finally. "He left before I could give him a message for Farrel. You ride in and tell Fat to take the usual precautions; tell him some of the Dog Town crowd are riding into Vaca tonight."

Compton nodded and stretched to his feet. "I'll tell Fat," he said quietly. "After dinner I think I'll take a nap; I've been losing considerable sleep lately."

Compton was the first to leave the cook shack. Yancey got up at the same time, and Burke watched the two younger men walk to the bunk-house. They were pulling off their boots when he entered and watched them speculatively.

"You gents working tonight?" he asked Compton.

"Yeah," Compton answered shortly. "The boss wants us to ride the outside circle and see if we can find that leak where he is losing beef."

"I should be doing something to earn my keep," Burke said slowly. "I'll ride with you and Skid."

"It's okay with me, if the boss does not object," Compton said carelessly, but the expression on Skid Yancey's face was clue enough for Burke.

"You're a poor liar, Charley," Burke said quietly.

"And Skid would make a poor poker player. Out with it now. Where are you two gun-hawks going tonight?"

"The only smart hombre in this whole set-up is Swifty Matthews," Compton said sullenly. "He sleeps out with the hoot-owls, and he don't have to answer any questions!"

"Lay your hackles, cowboy," Burke answered soothingly. "I'll stay here and keep Saint John busy. See that your gun does not hang after the ride to town, and don't throw off your shots. You should know better than to try to fool me by now!"

"Thanks, Stingaree," Compton said gratefully, and he crawled under a blanket.

Compton had the ability to relax, and he was soon sound asleep. Skid Yancey watched the face of Stingaree Burke for a time, and then crawled under his blanket. Burke went back to a little table where he used an apple box for a chair, and busied himself with some papers. He saw Shorty Benson leave the ranch on a fast horse, and ride off to the east. Then Ace Fleming dropped in and took a seat on a nearby bunk.

"That Rancho Vallejo graze," Fleming said carelessly, and in a low voice so as not to disturb the two sleepers at the other end of the room. "Some of it is pretty wild."

"That's right," Burke agreed. "Pretty much like

that badlands graze back around Lost River."

"How many head of Circle F steers did you see back there," Fleming asked bluntly, "when you were making a range-tally?"

Burke jerked up his head. Fleming was staring at some papers on the little table, and Burke also looked. He smiled coldly when he saw the Circle F brand opposite some figures.

"Sixty-odd head," Burke answered without hesitation. "Perhaps forty head of Box B stuff, and a sprinkling of S Bar S."

"All three of those brands are registered up here," Fleming said slowly. "I wonder how they got there?"

"They were unloading at a siding thirty miles from Laredo," Burke answered. The shipping point was from Saint George, Utah."

"So that gives me an active interest in your business," Fleming declared. "Not counting the treasure."

"There's no argument there," Burke agreed. "You make a better friend than an enemy, Ace."

"Both of us, Stingaree," Fleming answered. "Now tell me straight. How much chance has Charley got against Brett Slagle?"

Here were two men who could read sign with the best. Both were also inveterate gamblers, and men of proved courage. Burke studied the papers on the table with unseeing eyes.

"It will be mighty close," he said at last. "Charley

has one little thing in his favor, and it might be enough. Charley is right, while Slagle is dead wrong!"

## CHAPTER TEN

Charley Compton rode through the long twilight with Skid Yancey, heading for Three Points, and the road to Vaca. Neither had much to say, but each was busy with his thoughts. Two miles from the Circle F, they met a Box B cowboy who carried a rifle across his knees. A mile farther they met an S Bar S puncher similarly armed. When they saw a third cowboy evidently making a patrol, Compton spoke briefly to his saddle pard.

"Ace Fleming has spread the word, Skid. Every cattle outfit in these parts seems to be sending reps to guard against bushwhackers. You know what that means."

"Means Ace is afraid Pug Jones is sending a force of his gunfighters over from Dog Town," Yancey answered promptly. "Means we are going to have some law and order in these parts while Saint John is making medicine with Stingaree back on the Circle F."

He rode closer to Compton and lightly touched his shoulder. Compton looked up with a question in his eyes.

"Just wanted to touch a working cowboy worth five

thousand dollars," Yancey explained with a grin. "Now I can tell my grandchildren about it a bit later."

They passed Three Points and rode up the road leading to Vaca. Compton smiled as he stopped in front of the adobe jail.

"Our horses will be safer down here," he suggested. "It's less than a block to the Casino."

A string of horses were tied to the rails in front of the Casino; the long saloon was crowded when Compton and Yancey shouldered through the swinging bat-wing doors. They stopped at the curve of the bar near the front doors, and Tim Kelly glanced at them and raised his eyebrows inquiringly.

"Whiskey straight for me," Yancey said slowly.

"Small beer," Compton gave his order.

"He hasn't got here yet," Kelly said just under his breath. "Three of his pards are down at the far end of the bar. Watch yourself for a cross-fire!"

Compton nodded, dropped his right hand, and loosened his six-shooter against crimp. It had been three years since his last meeting with Brett Slagle; it seemed like only a few weeks ago.

Yancey downed his drink and poured a chaser of the same. Ace Fleming sat in the lookout's chair back in the gaming room. A tall cowboy stood near the back door where he could see the entire barroom.

"That's Charley Saunders of the S Bar S," Yancey

whispered to Compton. "Him and Ace cleaned up one gang of owl-hooters here several years ago. We ain't doing so bad."

He stiffened when the swinging doors swished violently. A tall man slipped swiftly inside, placed his broad shoulders against the front wall, and waited for his eyes to shed the light. Charley Compton was watching the stranger in the back-bar mirror.

Skid Yancey knew without telling that Brett Slagle had arrived. Slagle was about thirty, lean and muscular, and undeniably handsome. He wore the crossed belts of the two-gun man; both holsters were thonged low and toed-in for a fast draw.

Slagle saw Compton; their eyes met in the mirror. Compton nodded his head without turning. Two other men entered the saloon and ordered drinks from Fat Farrel. Then Slagle left the front wall and walked down the long room. He stopped near the center of the bar, ordered whiskey straight, and pushed his 5 X Beaver Stetson to the back of his head.

Gospel Cummings came in from the alley and stood beside Charley Saunders. A half-hour passed.

Brett Slagle ordered another drink. He played with it for a moment before raising the shot glass to his lips. Then he pushed away from the bar, wiping his lips with the back of his left hand.

"This is going to be different," he stated clearly.

"Somebody in this room is going to die tonight!"

Ace Fleming holstered his guns and watched the handsome stranger. Charley Compton placed his glass of beer on the bar and pushed clear. The drinkers along the bar moved to the back wall, watching the two gun-fighters who turned to face each other, and both were smiling.

"It's been three years, Compton," Slagle said quietly, but every man in the crowded room could hear him plainly. "Three years and about five hundred miles ago."

"Seems like yesterday," Compton answered. "I never had much time for a bounty hunter, Slagle!"

"You strangers stay out of this," Slagle said, without turning his head. "I don't need any help, and Compton don't want any!"

"That's reading my mind," Compton agreed in a low drawl. "You all talked out?"

"I'm ready," he said clearly.

Charley Compton saw the fine spray of wrinkles appear suddenly at the corners of Slagle's eyes. He struck down for his six-shooter just as Slagle made his bid. Orange flame lanced across the mahogany bar from two directions as six-shooters roared a stuttering duet.

The front window shattered just behind and a little to the left of Charley Compton. He caught his bucking gun high and eared back on the recoil for a follow-up.

Brett Slagle took a backward step and a little to the left. His mouth popped open; a startled expression appeared briefly in his slate-colored eyes as the message from his punctured heart reached his brain. The smoking six-shooter tumbled from his hand to the dirty sawdust on the splintered planking. Slagle swayed forward as his knees buckled suddenly. Then he was face down in the sawdust with his polished boots rattling out the last seconds of a futile life.

A garish light suddenly was reflected into the saloon from the street. Two piles of trash had been kindled and were burning brightly. The flat bark of a rifle came from out in the street, followed almost instantly by an answering fusillade. Then the thunder of hoofs as a dozen horsemen raced out of the shadows, and men from the saloon ran out through the back door into the alley to join the fight against the Dog Town raiders.

Gospel Cummings stood with his back to a wall, his twin six-shooters covering the gunmen against the wall. Tim Kelly held his position behind the bar with his scatter-gun eared back and ready to go.

Compton and Yancey went through the back and ran around the side of the adobe saloon to take a position behind some beer kegs near the street. Rifles barked flatly as hidden cowboys poured a withering fire after the racing horsemen.

In five minutes it was all over. Several horses were down in the wide street; here and there a man was lying motionless in the deep dust. The two fires were blazing brightly to warn the raiders against a return attack.

Charley Compton ejected the spent shells from his six-shooter; thumbed fresh cartridges from his gun-belt, and pushed them through the loading gate, with his hammer set on half-cock. Then he holstered the balanced weapon and went back into the saloon. Ace Fleming met him just inside the door.

"Feeling better?" the dapper gambler asked.

A little man carrying a black bag pushed through the front doors of the Casino. He glanced at Fleming with a nod, went directly to the body of Brett Slagle, and made a brief routine examination.

"Right through the heart," he stated. "Death was almost instantaneous. Who did this homicide?"

"I did, Doc," Compton said slowly. "The name is Charley Compton, and I work for the Circle F. He called for showdown; he got it!"

"At least thirty witnesses, Doc," Fleming added. "How many down outside?"

"Five dead and two more probables," Doc Craig growled. "Two wounded, but able to ride, not counting that pair you sent down shortly after dark. What the devil happened here tonight?"

"Dog Town raiders," Fleming explained briefly.

"Saint John threatened to burn Dog Town to the ground. It looks like Pug Jones meant to beat him to it!"

"Where is the law?" the doctor asked testily.

"Out on the Circle F," Fleming answered with a faint smile curling his lips.

The doors burst inward under the thrust of a powerful shoulder. John Saint John stood framed in the doorway with a six-shooter in each big hand.

"Every man in this room is deputized to help the law!" he roared. "We'll get right over to Dog Town and jail that whole outfit. Hold up your right hands!"

Tim Kelly coughed from behind the bar. His scatter-gun was trained on the big deputy; his deep voice was gruff when he spoke.

"The late Mister Law," he said grimly. "Well, better late than never, I always say. I'll vouch for Compton; I saw the whole play. Self-defense, and thirty witnesses to testify that Slagle called for showdown!"

"And who might you be?" Saint John asked coldly.

"Deputy U. S. Marshal with a roving commission," Kelly answered quietly. "I've been looking for Slagle for a year. He killed a lawman down in Texas, but I couldn't extradite him from up here. You want to make something out of it, Deputy?"

"I figured you for a law-dog," Saint John said more quietly. "I could use some help up here right now. Glad to have you, and you can work out of my office, and under my orders!"

Kelly answered bluntly. "Now get this straight, Saint John. I have my orders, and I'm taking none from you. Your office is local, and you've got plenty to do. Notify the coroner, call the meat wagon, and make out your reports. Get those dead men off the street before they start to drawing flies. That should keep you busy for quite a while, and satisfy even your sense of importance!"

"Don't try to tell me how to do my law work!" Saint John bellowed. "I haven't seen your credentials, so get them out pronto, Mister!"

Kelly flipped back his white apron. A five-pointed badge was pinned to his vest. He reached into an inside pocket of his vest and produced a thin flat wallet. He opened it and laid it on the bar.

"Can you read?" he asked Saint John dubiously. "No matter; there's my picture on my credentials. Give a look, big fella!"

Charley Compton watched and listened with interest. He glanced up and saw Ace Fleming watching him closely. Fleming jerked his head slightly, and Compton walked over to the bar.

"You knew Kelly was a law-dog?"

Compton nodded. "He was, when I was a ranger," he answered. "Up here I didn't ask any questions."

"How about you?" Fleming asked softly.

"I'm clean," Compton answered without hesitation. "No law badge."

They left the Casino and walked to the tie-rail. Skid Yancey had brought up the horses from in front of the jail; he was watching with interest as Boot Hill Crandall and his helper cleaned up the littered street. They were placing the dead raiders in a long black wagon, stopping at each crumpled heap to avoid the labor of carrying the deceased.

Fleming told Skid Yancey to help in town and to meet them at Three Points in an hour. Then he rode down the street with Compton.

Gospel Cummings was seated at his table when the two men tied up at the rail and halloed the house. The open Bible was before Cummings when they entered the cabin at his invitation. Charley Compton sat down on a bunk; Fleming took the one extra chair.

"I figured Kelly for a lawman," Cummings said quietly, and with no preliminaries. He looked squarely at Compton.

"How about Swifty Matthews?"

"I don't get you," Compton evaded. "What about Swifty?"

Gospel Cummings sighed. "This is the first time I've known you to pull that dodge," he chided. "Now listen to me, Charley. One day we were making a pasear back toward Lost River. We saw four men riding in from the east. Two of them were

Stingaree Burke and Tim Kelly. Another was your friend Swifty Matthews. Now let's start all over. How about Swifty Matthews?"

"I've told you all I know," Compton answered irritably. "Matthews was a ranger the same time I was. He is wanted in Texas, but they can't touch him up here!"

"Kelly is a Deputy U. S. Marshal with a *roving* commission," Cummings said. "He can take a criminal anywhere he finds him!"

"Swifty Matthews is not a criminal," Compton defended his old friend. "He killed Joe Demingway in self-defense."

"Like you killed Brett Slagle," Cummings said sadly. "And for the same reason. To see who was the fastest!"

Ace Fleming listened and made no comment. He had seen Gospel Cummings confound more than one man with his logic; he had heard Cummings say that Charley Compton was uncommonly good at reading sign. Compton faced Cummings with a little crease between his eyes.

"I had trouble with Slagle when I was wearing a law badge," he stated clearly. "Matthews had resigned from the Rangers when he had that run-in with Joe Demingway."

"You and Matthews made a good team when you were working together, from what I hear," Cummings continued. "We talked some about pieces to this puzzle, and you admitted the pieces were falling into place."

"Some of them are," Compton growled.

"The rest of them are bound to," Cummings insisted. "Stingaree Burke is a lawyer; Tim Kelly is a deputy marshal. Matthews is wanted in Texas. We saw them three riding together, making war on Cord Demingway and his gang. That tell you anything, Charley?"

Charley Compton sat up straight. A startled gleam appeared in his narrowed eyes as he bit down on his teeth.

"You old swamp coon," he accused Cummings. "You leave a big enough trail to follow. Tim Kelly could have arrested Swifty, and released him on his promise to surrender at some future time. Stingaree knows all the legal angles; it must have been his suggestion. Then all three of them work together to clear up this treasure mystery, and if they do, things will be changed a lot down in Texas!"

"Son, that's reading sign with the best," Cummings praised. "But it goes further than that. You stopped thinking too soon."

Charley Compton frowned again. "You and Swifty and I made a good team at one time," he repeated, and then he glared at Cummings. "I won't do it!" he said angrily. "And you know why!"

"The triangle can wait," Cummings reminded. "The way I see it, three mighty good men are working hard to help a girl. They are all risking their lives. That says just as plain as day that the girl comes first. Am I right?"

"Right as rain, you blasted old prairie law-sharp," Compton admitted bitterly.

"Tell him, Ace," Cummings said to Fleming. "It might save you trouble later."

"This trouble was brought up here to me," Fleming said quietly. "I always meet trouble halfway. I'm not too proud to accept all the help I can get when I need it. No man should be."

"Get down to cases, boss," Compton said gruffly.

"Swifty Matthews is going to live at the Circle F," Fleming announced quietly. "He is out there now!"

Charley Compton stared with his mouth open. Then his shoulders sagged as he stared at the toes of his scuffed boots.

"A man couldn't ask for a better pard to side him," Compton finally admitted grudgingly. "After all, neither Swifty or me count right now. We haven't been very good friends for a year or more, but I'll work with him if you say so. I can take orders!"

"Spoken like a man, and a Texan," Cummings praised quietly. "Now what about that map you lost?"

"That," Compton said with a shrug. "I have it in

my head. I could draw another one without half trying."

"Did you?" Cummings asked.

This time Compton made no attempt to evade the issue. "I did not," he answered. "They got the real map!"

Gospel Cummings nodded. "You had some good reason," he guessed shrewdly. "It will come out in good time."

"I'm through talking," Compton announced sullenly. "You ready to ride?" he asked Fleming.

"As soon as Skid Yancey gets here," Fleming answered.

"So he's out at the rail now," Compton growled. "I'll wait outside."


## CHAPTER ELEVEN

Pug Jones sat in the office behind the Red Rose Saloon. An expensive Stetson was pushed to the back of his nearly bald head, a thick cigar clenched tightly between yellowed teeth. The twin six-shooters were tied low on his thick legs, and while he was without a coat, a bandolier of rifle cartridges was slung across his chest, resting on his right shoulder.

Three hard-faced strangers sat in chairs watching the man who had sent to Laredo for them. All were notorious gun-fighters, jealous of each other and of Jones, but they had one thing in common. All were wanted by the law, and needed money for a getaway to some haven like South America.

"You saw my men when they high-tailed it back here from Vaca," Jones snarled at his hirelings.

"They just rode over there without a plan," one of the strangers remarked. "They got shot to ribbons."

"This time I have a plan," Jones said more quietly. "How many men did you boys bring up with you?"

"Nine, not counting us," Dude Fargo answered for his companions. "That makes twelve. How many have you left, Pug?"

"Ten I can count on," Jones replied. "Now here's the set-up. The Syndicate wants that land grant; it's supposed to be with the old Vallejo treasure. We get the loot, and all they want is that land-grant."

"Let's wipe out your old friend Demingway, and get the treasure!" Dude Fargo said callously.

"You're new in these parts, Dude," Jones said quietly. "Demingway has quite a gang, and they also have a map telling where the treasure is buried. They plan to get it and light a shuck by way of Saint George, Utah. We'll hit them from that end; I have an idea the law will bottle Demingway up from this end."

"So we'll have Demingway in the middle," Fargo

said with a smile. "When are we riding?"

"Within an hour," Jones said coldly. "I've sent pack horses ahead with provisions and extra ammunition. We will circle north above the cave, and hit them from a pass they will have to use to make a getaway!"

It was midnight when the four men left the Red Rose to walk to the big livery stable. A group of roughly dressed men were lounging inside the barn. They looked Pug Jones over with interest, and the boss of Dog Town studied each man carefully.

"I've got one change of fresh horses," he said to Fargo. "I'll have a couple of the boys bring these other horses along slowly. We might need them after the fight, just in case any of those Demingway owl-hooters slip out of the trap."

Pug Jones was a big man; he sat his saddle with a deep seat, his rifle across his knees. He took the lead and rode across the rangeland at a dog trot, keeping to the brush to avoid being sky-lined, and setting a course west by north. After a time they left the foothills and began a steady climb which took them above the highest reach of Lost River Cave. Only the soft chime of spurs and the creak of saddle-leather told of their passing, but when they had gone, a lone rider left a spur of rocks which served for a look-out peak.

Pug Jones led his party down a gradual slope and

called for a halt in a grassy flat near a brawling stream. He glanced at Dude Fargo and spoke gruffly.

"Back of us is the trail to Utah," he explained. "Up in front is the west entrance to Lost River Cave. Put the horses under a guard and get ready for the fight. We're going into the tunnel if we can make it, and if we can't, we'll blast our way inside!"

"Is this Lost River?" Fargo asked curiously.

Jones nodded. "It gets lost underground where it runs through the cave," he explained. "If we get inside before daylight, be careful. Some of those drops are better than a hundred feet."

Only the fading starlight gave enough illumination to distinguish the rocky banks of the little river as the men followed Jones and Fargo toward the west entrance to the tunnel. Jones sent one of his men ahead to reconnoiter, and five minutes later they heard the flat bark of a rifle.

"Let's get up there," Jones whispered. "Keep to cover, and don't let a man escape!"

Jones cursed softly when his scout failed to return. They found the man sprawled in the trail-side bracken with a bullet through the head. Pug Jones stared at the dead man, his swarthy face convulsed with rage.

"They know we're here now," he growled, and then he faced the forbidding entrance to the tunnel. "Every man cut loose a full magazine right into that tunnel!" he ordered. "Then reload and get ready to charge!"

Twenty men laid down a withering blast of fire, emptying their rifles as fast as they could pull trigger and work the levers. No answering volley came from the cave, and sweating hands worked feverishly to reload as the echoes rattled back from the rimrock high above. Pug Jones was the first man in the trail as he gave the order to attack.

"Follow me, you rannies. A man can't die but one time!"

Dude Fargo led his own men a little to the right. Pug Jones came charging from the left with his Dog Town fighters. An oppressive silence beat down after the furious barrage of rifle-fire. The silence was broken when a dozen rifles answered from the tunnel when the raiders were fifty yards from the entrance.

Four men went down under the hail of bullets, but the rest continued their mad charge. Now their rifles were barking savagely as Jones gave the order to seek cover.

The first fingers of dawn were plucking at the eastern sky as the rival outlaw gangs blasted at each other until the rifle barrels grew too hot to hold. Pug Jones was crouching near Dude Fargo; he cocked his shaggy head to the side and listened intently.

"Firing from the east," he remarked with a hard, crooked smile. "That would be the law from Vaca."

"What law?" Fargo asked. "You mean that big deputy sheriff?"

"Him, and a jasper who used to tend bar for me in the Silver Dollar," Jones answered sullenly. "Hombre by the name of Tim Kelly, and he's a deputy U. S. Marshal!"

"You never told me the outside law had moved in," Fargo said angrily.

"I only found out tonight," Jones growled. "Let's move up closer before the light gets too strong. Chances are Demingway will have to pull some of his men back to fight the law. He's like a prairie dog trying to watch two holes at the same time!"

The light faded to signal the end of the brief false dawn. Three men were inside the tunnel when the sun slanted over the eastern mountain some five minutes later. One of the three was Pug Jones. His rifle barked when a head raised up from behind a limestone rock. The man screamed and fell, and three more slugs crashed into his body to bring him a quick and merciful death.

Rifles began to answer from the dark interior of the long tunnel, and a man behind Jones gasped to tell of a mortal wound. Another man took his place as the Dog Town men wormed their way through the darkness. A snarling voice rose above the blasting of the rifles.

"Get out or get killed, Jones. Cord Demingway talking!"

Pug Jones triggered his rifle at the direction from which the voice had sounded. "Go to blazes!" he answered. "You're in a tight, Demingway!"

Rifles blasted to answer his challenge, and the damp air of the cave was heavy with the fumes of burning powder. The battle settled down to a sniping duel with neither force being able to see the other.

Cord Demingway left four men to hold back the Dog Town raiders. He made his way along the twisting tunnel to the east end where five men were engaging the forces from Vaca. He faced the large opening to the cave, his face twisted with rage.

Back in the cave in a line with the opening, he could see a great pile of dirt. Picks and shovels were lying near a large deep hole where they had been dropped at the first alarm given by the outside look-out.

"Curse 'em!" Demingway croaked hoarsely. "Another two hours and we would have had the loot and been gone!"

"We didn't find any loot, boss," a bearded outlaw said sullenly. "We dug down ten feet like that old map said, and all we hit was some old rotting timbers those old Spaniards used to shore up the diggings. Somebody else must have beat us to it!"

"We didn't dig deep enough!" Demingway raged. "Now they've got us boxed in here like gophers, with both ends blocked off!

"I know a way," Demingway continued slowly. "Hold them back, and watch that lower trail!"

He slid back into the deeper darkness near the deep hole his men had dug. Using the pile of dirt for a ladder, the outlaw climbed to a ledge about six feet above the floor of the cave. He moved back until he touched a damp wall of rock, and then Demingway began to climb slowly in the stygian darkness.

This was the old chimney of Lost River Cave, found by Gospel Cummings some five years previous, during a bear hunt. It was no longer a secret; every one in Vaca knew of the chimney entrance where only one man could crawl through at a time. Now it was used by the thousands of bats which lived in the cave; most of them had returned from their nocturnal hunting.

Cord Demingway made his way slowly upward, using the rocky sides of the chimney for footing. He paused when he saw a faint light above him; held his breath while he listened intently.

He could hear the faint explosions of guns from far down the trail, facing the front entrance to the cave. Then he started climbing again, stopping when his head was level with the top of the rocky chimney.

The minutes passed slowly while Demingway recovered his breath, and now he could hear every vagrant sound. Birds were singing in the trees on the high slope; they would have been silent if anyone were moving in the vicinity.

The tall outlaw pushed erect and climbed from the secret entrance. The first thing he did was twitch his twin six-shooters against holster crimp, after his long upward climb. A smile curled his lips as he turned to face the steep trail leading to the east. The smile froze instantly on the handsome outlaw's face.

"Howdy, Demingway," a deep voice greeted the outlaw. "Took you long enough to get here!"

"Swifty Matthews!" the answer came jerkily. "And you didn't grab a sneak!"

"I don't need a sneak," Matthews said quietly. "You're at the end of the trail, Demingway. Looks like you were going to run out on your boys!"

Demingway swore huskily. "You're on the dodge the same as me!"

"For killing your brother Joe, remember?" Matthews said.

Anger slows up the muscles, and for a moment Cord Demingway's eyes were almost closed. Swifty Matthews waited with his right hand hooked in the belt above his holstered six-shooter. Then he spoke softly.

"You didn't find the treasure, Cord. I'd have killed you if you had found it!"

Cord Demingway went into a crouch. Then he hesitated as curiosity got the better of him.

"You'd never have known," he sneered.

"I was watching," Matthews said coldly. "I got down into the cave the same way you came up. I saw your men digging like slaves, and following every direction of that old map!"

"You're a liar!" Demingway spat savagely.

"Pass that for now," Matthews said with a shrug. "I was down there when the look-out at the west entrance saw one of Pug Jones' men sneaking up. Then the law began to shoot from this end. You took it on the run for the west entrance, and I came on up the chimney to wait. You satisfied now?"

"Sorry I called you out of your name," Demingway said promptly. "Now it's between you and me."

"One minute," Matthews interrupted quickly. "You were heading for South America. Where did you cache the gold from that pocket your boys were working?"

Cord Demingway crouched with both hands poised above his holsters. "Mebbe you found the cache too?" he suggested.

Matthews nodded slightly. "I found it; it belongs

to Ace Fleming. Well?"

"All this talk must lead some place," Demingway answered quickly. "Where?"

"You've taken up for your brother, Joe," Matthews reminded softly. "I said Joe rubbed an ace off the bottom of the deck, and he went for his iron first. You and him are cut from the same piece of cloth. Any time you are ready!"

"If you win, you've got nothing to lose," Demingway said craftily. "If I win, the gold won't do you any good. You moved it?"

Matthews nodded. "I moved it, about twenty-odd pounds!"

"A little short of five thousand," Demingway said quietly. "Enough to get me a start in the Argentine. You want to play it that way?"

"That's the way I figured it," Matthews admitted. "Just remember I had you under my gun twice, and I didn't shoot!"

"I'll remember," Demingway promised. "I've waited a long time to square up for Joe. I always knew I was the fastest!"

"Gun proud," Matthews commented dryly. "I've got the same disease. I always knew I had you faded with an even break."

A six-shooter roared suddenly from not too far away. Both men were trained gun-fighters, fast and deadly with the tools of their trade. Two right hands dipped down as though motivated by the same impulse. Two shots roared out in a thunder of sound.

Swifty Matthews was jerked to the left and thrown to the ground as though struck by a mighty hammer. Cord Demingway took a quick step backward; then he went down with the smoking gun dropping from his nerveless hand. Silence for a moment,, and then Swifty Matthews coughed and sat up weakly. He turned his head when the sound of boots scuffed behind him.

"Take it easy, Swifty!" a voice called hoarsely. "It's Skid Yancey!"

Swifty Matthews grunted and turned slowly to face the Circle F cowboy. "That was you who gave the go-ahead," he said.

"That was me," Yancey admitted. "You both said all you wanted was a fair shake with no advantage on either side. You hurt bad?"

"Naw," Matthews answered weakly. "Broken left arm, is all. "What about Demingway?"

"Boot Hill waits for that owl-hooter," Yancey said coldly. "He asked for it, and he had it coming."

"Judge not lest ye be also judged," a deep voice interrupted solemnly. "Let this be a lesson to all of us. The wages of sin is—"

"Boot Hill," Yancey finished dryly. "Where did you come from?"

"I tracked your sign, son," Cummings answered

gravely. "You followed Swifty Matthews up here, or led the way. After I had told you that everyone in the Strip knew of this entrance through the chimney."

"Because you told Skid," Matthews corrected. "I did a little sign-reading on my own. With two forces closing in on Demingway, I figured sooner or later he'd be coming up through the hole. He did."

"Now he's ready to go down in another one," Skid Yancey added maliciously. "Don't let's stand here, Gospel. Swifty has been shot up bad; he's got a broken left wing!"

Skid Yancey went to the body of Cord Demingway, closed the sightless eyes, covered the face with the outlaw's Stetson, and unbuckled the crossed gunbelts. With these over his left arm, Yancey followed Cummings and Matthews down the steep path.

Shooting broke out from the valley as they reached the place where the horses browsed in a 'squite thicket. Gospel Cummings reached to his saddlebags and handed a quart bottle to Matthews.

"Take a bit of this anesthetic," he suggested. "If I get that slug out now, you won't have infection. Can you take it?"

Matthews took the whiskey bottle and drank a deep draught. "A cowboy can't stand on one leg," he said jocularly, and took another long swig. Then he handed the bottle back to Cummings and presented his left arm.

"Dig it out, Gospel," he said quietly. "Pay no mind to me if I yell my head off like a button!"

"Lie down," Cummings said gruffly.

He went to work with his probe, worked swiftly, and sighed with relief when the bit of lead dropped in the grass. Cummings swabbed the bleeding wound with permanganate, made a neat compress and bandage, and shook his head.

"I'm not a killer," Cummings said slowly. "I'll ride back with you, and fetch a doctor from town.

"Yancey," Matthews said slowly, "tell Charley Compton not to worry about Cord Demingway. Tell him I only got a scratch."

"I'll tell him," Yancey answered, and mounted his horse.

Cummings and Matthews rode down the trail and headed east and south for the Circle F. Skid Yancey tied his horse in a clump of creosote bush where Shorty Benson was guarding the Circle F horses, and complaining profanely because he was missing the fight.

"Relieve me so I can burn powder," he begged Yancey.

"I'd do it, but I got a message for Charley," Yancey answered importantly. "Swifty Matthews just killed the outlaw boss up near the chimney."

"Which one?" Benson asked tartly. "Demingway or Jones?"

"Cord Demingway; Swifty got shot up pretty bad."

He went up the path, keeping to cover as rifles blazed from the mouth of the big cave. Deputy Saint John bellowed for him to get down in the brush, and then Charley Compton called from behind a huge boulder.

"Whose hardware you got there?" Compton asked, and then he stared hard at the twin six-shooters. "Cord Demingway is dead," he said positively. "Who did for him?"

"Your pard," Yancey answered. "Gent by the name of Swifty Matthews. Swifty got shot some in the left arm, and old Gospel rode back to the Circle F with him. Said for you not to worry."

Tim Kelly came from behind a rock with a smoking rifle in his blocky hands. Saint John had wormed his way for a meeting, and Kelly spoke to the big deputy sheriff.

"Now is the time, lawman," he said quietly. "Pug Jones and just about every man he could hire is attacking the Demingway gang from the west. Let's you and me ride over to Dog Town and do what has to be done. We can't do much here."

"Don't tell him how to do his law work," Compton said with a wink at Kelly, before Saint John could speak.

"You've got a good idea there, Marshal," Saint John surprised the other two men. "Cole Brighton and Ace Fleming each sent a wagon over to Dog

Town to take the women and their gear to the rail station at Caldwell Junction."

Two hours later they quickened their pace when a column of smoke rose high in the air toward the east. They reached Dog Town just as two wagons left the burning town, loaded with women and their baggage. Old Cole Brighton of the Box B rode up to meet the two lawmen.

"Glad you got here, officers," the old cattleman said lamely.

"Yeah, you look like it," Saint John growled. "Who told you rannies to put the torch to Dog Town?"

"Our women folks," Brighton answered quickly. "And you know how the ladies are when they get a notion in their heads."

"Yeah, I know," Kelly answered. "They had a meeting yesterday over at the Circle F." He stared hard at Brighton and announced: "Cord Deming-way is dead!"

"The devil you whisper!" Brighton said in a startled voice. "Swifty or Charley?"

"Swifty; he got a broken left arm in the show-down!"

Brighton spoke up carelessly. "I cleaned out the desk in Pug Jones' office before we set it ablaze." He handed a pair of bulging saddle-bags to Kelly, and Saint John offered his usual protest.

"I'll take the evidence!"

"You won't," Kelly answered coldly. "Orders of the U. S. Marshal, and I'm repping for him. Let's get back to the Circle F."

## CHAPTER TWELVE

Stingaree Burke crawled through the brush, and stopped beside Charley Compton who was firing into the front entrance of the big cave. The old lawyer listened to the answering fire for a moment, and spoke confidently.

"Demingway don't have too many left," he commented.

"Demingway is dead," Compton answered curtly. "Swifty Matthews killed him, and got a broken left arm himself."

"I've been talking to Skid Yancey," the old lawyer said. "Sooner or later Pug Jones will be in command of the cave. We ought to be there to protect our interests."

"You mean down the chimney?" Compton asked.

"That's what I mean. We know about that secret entrance, but I don't believe Jones does. Want to take a chance?"

"The three of us," Compton agreed promptly. "You and me and Skid Yancey. Pass the word to Skid. I'll talk to Ace Fleming."

Burke withdrew into the deeper bracken, and

Compton made his way to a fort of rocks where Fleming was directing his Circle F men. The gambler listened while Compton outlined his plan. Fleming frowned, and then nodded in agreement.

"A man has to take chances," he said with his usual fatalism. "How will we know when to charge in?"

"Three fast shots in a row," Compton suggested. "We are getting close."

Compton crawled away and met Yancey and Burke at a bend in the rocky trail. Skid Yancey shucked his spurs, tightened his belt, and led the way up the steep trail. He paused at the place from where he had watched the duel between Demingway and Matthews.

"I'll take the lead down the chimney," he whispered. "We take it slow so as not to make any noise. There are little shelves of rock for a man to stand on. The place stinks of bats, but they won't hurt a man. If we make any noise, there might be a committee waiting for us when we step on the shelf down below."

"Bend the lead," Compton said tersely. "I'll be right after you, Stingaree will follow me."

Yancey climbed the last twenty yards to the top of the stone chimney. He hoisted his legs up and into the hole, disappeared from sight, and Compton followed him.

Charley Compton could hear the slither of Yancey's clothing against the sides of the chimney. He felt with each boot until he found a little rocky ledge, and then lowered the other foot. The light faded at the top; the stench of bat guano was stifling. Compton knew then that Burke had also entered the chimney, and was shutting off some of the precious air.

He worked his way down for what seemed an interminable time. A hand touched his leg lightly. A voice whispered softly close to his ear.

"Duck down and step to the left. We are on the shelf!"

Compton crouched, stepped to the left, and then he saw Yancey. The Circle F cowboy told him to warn Stingaree Burke, and Compton waited for the old lawyer to reach the shelf. A moment later the three men were huddled on the wide shelf above the floor of Lost River Cave. Occasionally a rifle would wink out from the darkness, and the roaring explosions echoed back from the high limestone walls.

Charley Compton waited until his eyes had become accustomed to the semi-gloom of the big cave. It was bright out toward the entrance, and two men were crouching behind huge stalagmites. The limestone pillars glittered like diamonds, and Compton saw them in countless numbers leading back into the dark forbidding recesses of the huge cave.

He leaned forward and stared at a great pile of

dirt on the floor beneath the shelf on which they rested. Stingaree Burke was also staring at the deep hole; he moved closer to Compton.

"The treasure?" he whispered.

"That's the location," Compton answered. "They didn't find the treasure."

"You knew they wouldn't," Burke whispered.

"Only two Demingway men left at this end," Compton changed the subject.

"We could get them like shooting fish in a barrel," Yancey said eagerly. "You take the one on the right; I'll rub out the one on the left."

"Hold it," Compton said quickly. "We'd give our position away, and I hear shooting from deep in the cave."

Silence for some minutes, broken only when a shot came from outside, and was answered by one of the outlaws at the mouth of the cave.

"Look yonder!" Yancey whispered hoarsely. "Three men sneaking up from the west end!"

"Those hombres in front should have warning," Compton grunted.

He picked up a clod, drew back his arm, and threw the clod across the cave. Both men whirled just as the three men coming from the west opened fire. One of the defenders went down, but he continued to fire his rifle from the floor.

"One of those three is Pug Jones!" Yancey whispered to Compton. "And he just lost a man!"

They could make out the squat figure of Jones outlined against the faint light from the lower end of the cave. The Dog Town outlaw fined his sights and pressed the trigger. The man at the front of the cave pitched to the limestone floor, his hot rifle falling from his grimy hands. His partner fired a shot, and a gasping gurgle came from back in the gloom. Then Pug Jones closed the battle with a final shot which silenced the wounded outlaw at the front of the cave.

Let's get down there," Compton whispered. "Keep behind cover, but leave Jones to me. You two guard that west tunnel in case some of his men find their way up here!"

He stepped to the pile of dirt and slid to the floor of the cave, followed by Burke and Yancey. All found refuge behind limestone pillars, watching for Pug Jones to come into the light.

Boots scuffed softly on the smooth floor, and a moment later the huge form of Pug Jones stepped into the light. He almost ran to the hole which the Demingway outlaws had dug. He carefully placed his rifle against a stalactite, went to his knees, and peered into the deep excavation.

"I better tell the boys," he said to himself, and pushed up to his feet.

"Better tell me first," Charley Compton spoke suddenly. "Don't reach for your hardware!"

"Compton!" the outlaw gasped, and then he saw

Charley Compton standing in the clear, watching him closely. He also saw that Compton was empty-handed, and Jones swelled his big chest.

"So you joined up with Cord Demingway," he sneered.

"Demingway is dead," Compton said grimly. "You and your men are surrounded, what's left of you. I'm giving you a chance to surrender!"

"You're giving me a chance?" Jones laughed raucously.

"Dog Town is burned to the ground," Compton said quietly. "Demingway is dead. Who's the head man in the Syndicate?"

"How did you get in here?" Jones countered.

"Down the chimney; you evidently never heard about that one!"

"My men will be up here soon," Jones warned. "Now I'll make you a proposition. Where's the Vallejo treasure?"

"There's the hole yonder," Compton answered. "They didn't find anything."

"I'll give you a cut," Jones offered. "One fourth if you find the treasure!"

"That treasure belongs to the heirs of old Don Alvarado Vallejo," Compton said simply.

"Finders keepers, I always say," Jones declared. "One fourth, and your life!"

"I've got my life," Compton said slowly.

Jones jerked up when two rifles boomed in the

tunnel behind him. They were answered by a return from farther to the west, and Compton smiled grimly.

"If you were stalling for time, you can get down to cases now," he stated. "You men will never get into the cave!"

"I'm giving you one more chance," Jones said arrogantly. "Throw in with me, find the treasure, and take a third!"

"No dice," Compton answered slowly. "Who's top man in the Syndicate?"

"I am," Jones answered proudly. "And I can find the treasure now without any help from you!"

"Demingway didn't find it," Compton pointed out. "And he had the original map."

He was watching Pug Jones intently. Jones had both big hands hooked into his gun-belts above the six-shooters in his twin holsters. Compton studied the thick-splatted fingers; shifted his gaze to the burly outlaw's face. He saw the fine spray of wrinkles wink out at the corners of the killer's mean little eyes. This was the go-ahead!

Compton dipped his right hand down and up, curling the hammer of his six-shooter back on the draw. Orange flame blasted from the muzzle of his leaping gun, followed almost instantly by a stuttering explosion as Jones drew and fired.

The two men faced each other across the open pit, and then Compton stood there alone. A sudden thump came from the deep hole; then all was still.

Charley Compton sighed and pointed his smoking gun at the floor. He triggered off three rapid shots, put his hammer on half-cock, and ejected the spent shells from his .45 Colt. Then he reloaded and holstered the smoke-grimed weapon deep in leather.

He was waiting at the cave entrance, but keeping behind cover, when Ace Fleming hailed him from down the trail.

"That you, Charley?"

"Come on up!" Compton shouted. "All clear at this end!"

Ace Fleming came running up the trail with six men. They crowded into the cave around Compton, who warned them to stay close to the walls.

"Stingaree and Yancey are holding the west tunnel." he explained. "Some of the Jones gang are still making a fight."

"Jones?" Fleming asked. "We heard pistol shots!"

"That pile of dirt back yonder," Compton said quietly. "Jones fell into that hole. He was looking for the treasure!"

"Listen!" Fleming cautioned. "I hear Stingaree Burke talking!"

"You Laredo men!" the voice of the old lawyer bellowed. "You better get out while you can. Pug Jones is dead, and most of his men. The law will close in on you at sundown!"

"We should have sent some men around to block that Saint George trail," Fleming said regretfully.

"We'll clear out," a muffled voice came faintly from down the dark tunnel, and then all was silent.

Stingaree Burke came into the light with his rifle at the ready. He slipped behind a limestone pillar when he saw the group of men in the cave. He emerged again when he recognized Fleming and the Circle F men.

"Howdy, Ace," he greeted the gambler quietly. "How many men did we lose?"

"Three wounded," Fleming answered gratefully. "Who did for these hombres here in the cave?"

"Pug Jones and his men," Compton answered. He turned to Burke and said: "I found out who was the head of the Syndicate!"

"Give him a name!" the old lawyer pleaded. "Some hombre from down Laredo way?"

His name was Pug Jones," Compton replied. "He told me so just before he made his play."

"Where is he?" Yancey asked, as he came from the tunnel.

"In that deep hole yonder. That's as close to the treasure as he ever got."

"Did they find it?" Burke asked eagerly.

"Let's make a pine torch and take a look," Compton suggested.

He went to a pile of rocks the outlaws had used for a fireplace. Compton chose a stub of pitch-pine, splintered it with the blade of his stock knife, and struck a match. With the torch blazing, he led the way to the deep hole and leaned over to peer down into the depths. The other men watched from both sides of the cave; they saw the huge bulk of Pug Jones lying motionless at the bottom.

"They cut notches in the side for a ladder," Compton said, as he pointed to a series of holes at one end of the deep hole. "I'm going down!"

Fleming took the torch while Compton climbed down into the pit. They watched as Compton took the torch and examined all sides of the excavation. The hole was about ten feet long, nearly as wide, and ten feet deep.

"What do you make of it, Charley?" Fleming asked eagerly.

"We ought to have a couple of ropes to get Jones out of here," Compton answered. "All I can see is some rotted timbers." He reached down and picked a piece of rusty metal from the side of the hole.

"What's that?" Yancey asked.

"Burro shoe, what's left of it after a hundred years," Compton answered. "Now we know how they packed the treasure up here."

He stuck the blazing torch in a crevice and climbed out of the hole. He looked about for Stingaree Burke, and the old lawyer came into the front of the cave. He was smiling eagerly, and holding something in his hand.

"I just went up to visit the late Cord Deming-way," he explained. "I found him where Matthews let him lay, and I also found this in that outlaw's pocket. Looks like a map!"

He was watching the face of Charley Compton as he spoke. Compton nodded his head with a little sigh.

"That's the map they stole from me," he admitted. "The original map drawn by old Don Alvarado Vallejo."

"Then all we have to do is read the map," Burke declared. "The writing is in Spanish, but I can make it out."

"It tells how to get to Lost River Cave," Burke continued. "So we don't have to bother with that. Now here we are inside the cave. It indicates three heavy pillars of limestone, and a wide shelf across the top. That would be where we came down from the chimney."

Charley Compton remained silent. He was watching Burke with a little smile framing his mouth. The old lawyer bent closer and continued to read the map. "Between the two end pillars," he read slowly. "Twenty-two paces from mouth of cave, due east and west."

He put a heel at the edge of the pit, paced slowly to the entrance of the cave, counting slowly. Then he retracted his steps, still counting.

"Cord Demingway had it right," he muttered.

"The map says ten feet down. They got down about that far."

Stingaree Burke climbed down into the pit and measured up with his hands. "A bit more than ten feet," he said slowly. "Either they found the treasure, or some hunter beat them to it!"

"If the treasure was ten feet down, it should be right under your feet," Fleming interrupted. "It would start at about ten feet. Some of you boys climb down there and start to dig!"

Three cowboys climbed into the hole and started digging. Charley Compton watched them work, but he made no move to join them. Stingaree Burke touched him on the arm and spoke in a low voice.

"What do you think, Charley? You know what this means to Mona Belle."

"Yeah, I know," Compton answered wearily. "Mebbe we didn't read that map just right. This is a big cave, and we know there is another entrance down at the west end of the tunnel."

"It would be dangerous to go down there right now," Burke objected. "Some of those Laredo owlhooters might be hanging around; they'd pick us off from the brush, or hide behind one of those limestone pillars."

"That treasure has been buried a hundred years," Compton said slowly. "A day or so more won't matter much. I'm thinking about the dead men that must be lying down there. What about them?"

"We will notify Saint John," Burke said brusquely. "Old Gospel will be busy for a while, if they pack all those owl-hooters back to Hell's Half Acre."

"They wiped each other out, those outlaws," Compton said slowly. "And by now Dog Town should be burned to the ground."

"The treasure," Burke insisted. "Seems to me you'd show more interest."

"What do you want me to do?" Compton asked irritably. "I've worked on this puzzle day and night. We can look some more after we all get some rest. We know the outlaws didn't pack it out, so it must be here somewhere!"

"I reckon you're right, rod," Burke agreed.

"What did you say?" Compton asked.

"Wasn't you ramrod of the Vallejo Rancho?" Burke asked testily. "You still are, if we prove ownership to the land!"

"Mebbe so; mebbe not," Compton answered curtly. "Mona Belle is the boss, and right now she is looking after Swifty Matthews!"

A slow smile began to spread across the old lawyer's smooth face. "So that's what is eating on your innards."

"Listen to those shovel-cowboys dig," Compton changed the subject, and they walked back to the pit. He looked down and watched the sweating cowboys swing picks and shovels. One of them yelled and stooped to pick up a glittering object.

"We've struck it!" he shouted. "It's a gold piece!"

Stingaree Burke climbed down in the pit and took the gold piece from the excited cowboy. The lawyer held the coin under the torch and swore softly under his breath.

"This is a twenty-dollar gold piece," he said scornfully. "Minted at Denver in the year 1883!"

"One of the outlaws must have dropped it out of his pocket," Compton suggested. "I'm heading back for the Circle F!"

Charley Compton left the cave and walked out into the bright sunlight. He headed down the steep trail, rounded a bend, and came to a bosque where Shorty Benson was guarding the horses.

"Did you find the loot?" Benson asked eagerly.

Compton shook his head. "One of the boys found a gold piece down in the hole," he answered. "Minted not many years ago, but they are still digging. I'm heading back for the Circle F."

"Well!" Benson muttered, as Compton climbed his saddle and headed east. "He don't seem very interested."

Charley Compton rode slowly, rolled a cigarette, and lighted his smoke. He inhaled deeply, and then a broad smile appeared on his bronzed face. After finishing his smoke, he reached to his saddlebags behind the cantle, and drew out a thick meat sandwich. He munched it slowly as he rode along, still smiling with obvious enjoyment. He rode into the

Circle F yard about two in the afternoon, stripped his riding gear, and turned his horse into a corral. Mona Belle called from the big house, and Compton hurried to her side.

"How's Swifty?" he asked softly.

"The doctor left not more than twenty minutes ago," the girl answered. "Swifty is sleeping now. What happened back there, Charley?"

"Most of the outlaws are dead," Compton explained. "Stingaree gave the rest a chance to light out for Utah."

"Pug Jones?" the girl asked hesitantly.

"He's dead," Compton answered gruffly. "I gave him a chance to surrender!"

Mona Belle asked no more questions. She knew the answers now as far as Demingway and Jones were concerned. Swifty Matthews had killed one of the leaders; Charley Compton had killed the other.

"The treasure?" she whispered. "Did they find it?"

Compton slowly shook his head. "I don't believe they are digging in the right place," he said quietly. "I was too tired to argue. Like I told Stingaree, that treasure has been there for a hundred years. A day or two more won't matter much."

Mona Belle watched his face closely. "That isn't like you, Charley," she said slowly. "Is there anything else you want to tell me?"

Charley Compton glanced around the big yard. He was about to speak when Sandra Fleming came out of the house.

"Some other time," Compton said irritably. "Now I'm going to wash and change clothes. I'll be in to see Swifty when he wakes up."

Mona Belle watched him stalk off to the bunk house. "Proud, stubborn fool," she said, and her teeth were clenched.

"All men are," Sandra Fleming said soothingly. "But I've learned one thing, Mona Belle. After a gun-fight, a man takes quite a while to get back to normal. Ace was always like that, so I just wait until he has adjusted himself."

"Do you think that could be it?" Mona Belle asked hopefully.

"I'm sure of it," Sandra assured the worried girl. "Swifty Matthews is in love with you—too," she said quietly.

Mona Belle turned quickly. "You're just guessing," she answered tartly.

"It is Charley you love," Sandra said softly.

"I didn't say it was!"

"You will be a very wealthy girl," Sandra continued. "That might make Charley tongue-tied."

"I won't have a thing unless the old land-grant is found," Mona Belle said worriedly. Then she began to smile. "I hope they don't find it," she said quietly. "Then I won't be a very wealthy girl. I wish something would happen to pound some sense into that jug-headed cowboy!"

"Perhaps something will," Sandra said. "There's Gospel Cummings waiting to talk to Charley."

Compton glanced up with a frown when Cummings called to him. He walked into the bunk-house and took off his brush-coat.

"It's all over but the planting," he told Cummings.

The tall plainsman frowned. "How many?" he asked sadly.

"Four wounded," Compton answered. "The deceased, about twenty, were all outlaws, so don't feel too bad. They killed each other; that is, all but the two leaders."

"Demingway and Jones," Cummings said slowly. "I know about Demingway, and you've smoked your gun. Jones?"

Compton nodded. "Jones wouldn't surrender," he explained. "Neither would I, so I did the best I could."

"The treasure," Cummings asked. "Off-hand I'd say they didn't find it."

"They didn't," Compton agreed. "Neither did the Circle F hands. They are still digging, but I came on in. I was a bit worried about Swifty."

"I was thinking about Mona Belle," Cummings said slowly. "When she gets her affairs all straightened out again, she will need a good man to ramrod the ranch down in Texas."

Compton regarded Cummings suspiciously. "Just

what are you driving at, old-timer?" he asked quietly.

"Love," Cummings answered promptly. "You don't drink a drop, you know cattle from hocks to horns, and that Vallejo graze. That little filly likes you a heap, you tongue-tied rannihan!"

"Mind your own business!" Compton blazed. "Mona Belle will be one of the richest girls in Texas. What am I? A working cowboy with a few sections of land!"

"Putting it that away, mebbe she won't get the ranch back," Cummings said slowly. "That would make you and her even. No land, no money, nothing but youth and beauty."

Charley Compton glared at Cummings, who stroked his luxuriant brown beard with apparent unconcern. Compton sat down on his bunk, drew his six-shooter and broke it down, and commenced to clean it thoroughly.

"Mona Belle will get the ranch back," he said finally, and his tone was positive.

"What makes you so sure?" Cummings asked.

"That's one of the missing pieces of the puzzle," Compton answered with an exasperating grin.

"Do me a favor, Charley," Cummings said hopefully. "When you go out to Lost River Cave again, I'd like to ride along with you."

Charley Compton frowned. "That's fine with me," he answered gruffly. "The four of us will ride out there tomorrow after breakfast."

"The four of us?" Cummings repeated.

"Stingaree and Mona Belle," Compton answered. "You and me makes four."

"What about Ace Fleming?" Cummings asked.

"So make it six," Compton shouted. "Ask Saint John!"

## CHAPTER THIRTEEN

The law rode into the Circle F yard, followed by a heavy wagon with a flat bed. John Saint John and Tim Kelly dismounted and off-saddled. Long Tom Brady tooled his four-horse hitch close to the house where Ace Fleming maintained his office. Charley Compton joined the two lawmen as they went to join Brady.

"We brought the effects of Pug Jones," Kelly explained to Compton.

"The late Pug Jones," Compton corrected. "He wouldn't surrender when I gave him a chance. Cord Demingway is likewise; Swifty Matthews is in the house with a broken left arm."

He told the story of the battle at Lost River Cave briefly. Kelly shrugged and pointed to the gear on the flat-bed.

"Let's carry this stuff into Fleming's office. It

should furnish several more pieces to that puzzle we have been working on."

Tom Brady had found two heavy stakes which he slipped under the safe between the legs. With two men on each side, they carried it into the office and deposited it in one corner.

"Jones was the head of the Syndicate," Compton told Kelly. "You should find the names of his associates among his papers."

"I found some of them," Kelly replied. "The big wheel seems to be John Fargo, more familiarly known as Dude. He was one of the witnesses against Swifty Matthews in that shooting case down at Laredo."

"I know the gent," Compton said with a nod. "He claimed that the Vallejo Rancho was in the Public Domain, and a lot of his gang filed homesteads on the lower end of the ranch along the Rio Grande."

"The Land Commissioner is looking into that," Kelly said slowly. "If we could find that old land grant, all those claims would be automatically nullified."

"You won't need me here, but I'll be around if you want me later," Compton said, and he left the office.

Mona Belle was waiting on the big front porch, and she beckoned for Compton to join her.

"Swifty is awake," she said in a low voice. "He's asking for you, Charley."

"I'll go right in," Compton answered. "About the treasure—will you ride over with us early in the morning?"

"Us? Who else is going?" the girl asked, and her face showed her disappointment.

"It got rather involved," Compton explained. "Gospel Cummings invited himself and Ace. Then there will be the law and Stingaree. We will leave right after breakfast."

Mona Belle seized Compton's right hand and held it tight. The light faded from her dark eyes as she leaned closer to Compton. "I am not sure that I want to be wealthy," she said with a little pout.

Charley Compton tightened his jaws, and then his left arm went around her slim waist. Mona Belle smiled and leaned against the strength of his deep chest. The door opened and Sandra Fleming beckoned to Mona Belle.

"Swifty is asking for you and Charley," she called.

Mona Belle sighed as Compton dropped his arm. "Le us go in," she said in a low voice. "There will be another time."

The brooding expression left the face of Charley Compton. He was smiling as they followed Sandra Fleming.

Swifty Matthews was lying on a low bed in a side

room. His left arm was in a splinted bandage, and his face was pale from loss of blood.

"Howdy, Charley," he greeted Compton. "Congratulations on a better job than I did. You didn't get hurt?"

"Not a scratch," Compton answered with a smile. "The law got back from Dog Town, and they brought all of the head man's effects here with them including his safe. Tim Kelly says that a lot of those witnesses against you down at Laredo were members of the Jones gang. That should mean acquittal for you on that old charge."

"Then I can come out of the brush again," Matthews said with a wan smile. "What about the treasure?"

"We didn't find it," Compton explained. "I have a hunch they were digging in the wrong place."

"I saw that pit," Matthews said thoughtfully. "It was right under the shelf, facing the entrance to the cave."

"Ace and Stingaree are digging back there right now," Compton said lightly. "Unless they give it up for today."

He paused as voices sounded outside. Ace Fleming came into the house with Stingaree Burke, and their clothing was dirty from digging. Burke appeared tired as he followed Fleming to the sick room.

"Did you find it?" Matthews asked eagerly.

"We went down another six feet," Burke answered with a sigh. "It's my belief that someone got there ahead of us. People have been searching for the Vallejo treasure for more than seventy years."

"We've got to find it," Matthews said grimly. "Or the Rancho Vallejo will be Public Domain!"

"It didn't seem to me like that earth had been disturbed recently," Fleming remarked.

"We will keep on looking if we have to dig up the entire cave," Stingaree Burke announced. "It's got to be twenty-two paces from some place in that cave, and ten feet down!"

Compton shook his head. "I've just got a hunch," he answered stubbornly. "According to old Jose Morales, the land agent was wrapped in oil silk, and sealed up in a small casket of sheet lead. It is much more valuable than all the treasure!"

"The treasure," Matthews said slowly. "Gold bullion and jewels. Jewels worth a King's ransom, according to the old tales. Worth a quarter of a million."

"Mona Belle will be wealthy if we find the treasure," Fleming said emphatically.

Mona Belle sighed and excused herself.

"Mona Belle cares little for money," Stingaree Burke said slowly. "But I never saw anyone love a home the way she loves Rancho Vallejo."

"Let's get over to the office and talk to the law," Ace Fleming suggested. "Let these two old saddle

pards visit for a while. Don't tire him out, Charley,"
he warned over his shoulder, as he and Burke left
the sick room.

Charley Compton watched them go, and then sat
down on a chair facing Matthews. They studied
each other for a moment. Matthews was the first to
speak.

"That triangle, Charley. I won't ever stop trying!"

Compton sat up straight, and his face darkened
with a surge of anger which he quickly controlled.
"I know," he said quietly. "It's like Gospel Cummings said that day in his cabin down at Three
Points."

"I disremember," Matthews protested. "What did
he say?"

"Mona Belle would be the final voice," Compton
reminded him.

"Sometimes I wish that shoot-out had been a draw
between Demingway and me," Matthews muttered.
"Then there would be no more triangle."

"I felt the same way about Pug Jones," Compton
growled. "It only gave speed to my hand!"

"Yeah," Matthews agreed. "Likewise. I'll be seeing you around!"

Compton left the room and headed for the bunk-
house. He stopped when Fleming called from the
office. Compton retraced his steps; stopped just inside the office where Tim Kelly was slowly working

the combination on the Dog Town safe.

"We found the combination in some papers," Fleming whispered. "Kelly ought to have it open in a minute."

"I have it!"

Kelly turned the knob and then swung the heavy door back. Saint John leaned forward as Kelly drew out some folded papers. After a brief examination, Kelly spoke quietly.

"Seems to be a list of names in that Syndicate," he explained. "Most of them are wanted by the law, and quite a few of them are dead now. Wait a minute!"

He leaned forward to read a soiled paper. "This is to Pug Jones from Joe Demingway," he said slowly. "He was one of the Jones' gang, and he says here that he will kill Swifty Matthews in a card game. You know what that means?" he asked.

"It clears Swifty of that old charge down in Laredo," Fleming answered quickly. "What are those tally sheets?"

"They seem to represent jags of cattle," Kelly answered. "And unless I am wrong, most of these cattle are grazing on the Box V right now. Two hundred head of Box B stuff, a hundred and fifty Circle F, and some odd brands they must have rustled here and there on the drive."

"What about money?" Fleming asked. "Jones was doing a good business over at Dog Town, and it should have been in cash."

Tim Kelly cleaned out the safe, and dumped books and papers on the floor.

"There is ten thousand dollars here, men," Kelly said slowly. "I will impound it to settle the debts of the estate. Such as compensation for rustled cattle, funeral expenses, and the like!"

"Which reminds me, Saint," Fleming said slowly. "We did part of your work for you. I sent a man to town to notify Boot Hill Crandall to pick up those outlaws."

"Well, thanks, and I take that kindly," Saint John answered.

The lawman made his farewells and went out to mount his big horse. Fleming stared after the big man and spoke quietly.

"I can't figure what got into the Saint," he said. "He hasn't asserted his importance now for going on three days."

"He was watching Tim Kelly," Compton said with a grin. "A boy always learns by example, and men are only boys grown tall."

Tim Kelly was studying some papers; he looked up with a frown. "I wonder if Dude Fargo is alive?" he said slowly. "Next to Jones, he seems to be the head man in that Syndicate."

"If Fargo is still alive, which I doubt, he should be halfway to Utah by now," Fleming said carelessly. "How bad is he wanted?"

Kelly frowned. "We know Fargo is mixed up in a lot of crooked deals, but we have no real evidence that would stand up in court," he replied. "If it so happened that he got hold of that old land grant, he could make Miss Courtney a lot of trouble."

"He won't make Mona Belle any trouble," Compton said emphatically.

Stingaree Burke turned to stare at Compton. "I wish you'd speak out, Charley," he said irritably. "You had that old map; got it from old Jose Morales the night he died. It was stolen from you, and Cord Demingway got it. He dug a deep pit according to the map, and you didn't seem a bit worried. You left us digging in the cave, and now you are leading another hunt tomorrow."

"Just a hunch," Compton said slowly. "You know how it is, Stingaree. If I'm wrong, I'll never hear the last of it. Let's wait until tomorrow."

"The last piece in the puzzle," Fleming said thoughtfully. "I'll bet old Gospel Cummings could read it from what we have now."

"Like as not he could," Compton agreed. "Did you bring the old map with you?"

"I have it in my wallet," Fleming said. He drew out his billfold, extracted the old map, and handed it to Compton.

"Thanks," Compton said. "I want to study it some more tonight."

"You don't need the map, from what I heard,"

Kelly said sternly. "You memorized that map in your head. But just go on being mysterious, Compton. I'll be waiting for you down at Laredo when you've finished up here."

"Be seeing you, marshal," Compton answered, and he left the office.

As Charley walked through the house Mona Belle came out of the sick room at the end of the hall. Her face was flushed, and she came to Compton when she saw him in the hallway. He looked at her closely, and tears filled her eyes.

Compton took her hands and drew her to him. His arms went about her, and Mona Belle sobbed as she clung to him.

"I didn't want to hurt him, but he insisted," she said in a choked voice.

"You mean Swifty?"

Mona Belle nodded. "He wanted me to marry him at once!"

"You mean he didn't wait until this thing was settled?" Compton asked. "You mean you told him no?"

Mona Belle nodded twice. Charley Compton tightened his arms. He nudged back her head with his square chin; looked deep into her dark eyes.

"I love you, Mona Belle," he whispered roughly. "We are both as poor as prairie dogs, but I'll work hard for you."

Mona Belle raised her head and listened. Then

she threw back her head until she could look into Compton's face.

"Is this a proposal?" she asked in a little voice.

"I'm asking you to marry me," Compton answered fiercely. "Mrs. Mona Belle Compton. You could go farther and do better, but I'll do the best I can!"

Mona Belle hid her face and tightened her arms. "When?" she whispered.

"You name the time," Compton said huskily. "Sometime soon?"

"Before we go back to Texas," Mona Belle whispered. "I'm so happy I could cry!"

"None of that." He winked at Mona Belle and tipped his Stetson at a jaunty angle. "I'll see you later, Mrs. Mona Belle Compton," he said happily. "I've got to see a man about a triangle!"

His face changed as he hesitated at the door to Swifty Matthews' room. Then he knocked, turned the knob, and went slowly in. He sat down in the chair near the bed, and regarded his old saddle pard for a long moment.

"I know," Matthews said gloomily. "Mona Belle told you!"

"Yeah, she told me," Compton admitted. "You knocked one point off the triangle."

Matthews tried to sit up. "What are you trying to say?" he asked roughly.

"I was going to wait until this thing was settled,"

Compton answered quietly. "After you tried your luck, I barged in and tried mine."

"And you got the same answer," Matthews said hopefully. "She was too worried to talk about it."

"Sometimes you don't have to talk much," Compton said slowly. "Sometimes actions speak louder than words!"

Matthews stared, and then his eyes lighted up. "You look happy," he whispered. "You mean she loves you?"

"Mrs. Mona Belle Compton—I like the sound of that name," Compton said slowly. "I wanted you to be the first to know."

## CHAPTER FOURTEEN

Charley Compton awoke with the first early rays of the sun tugging at his eyelids. He dressed quietly so as not to awaken the other sleepers in the bunkhouse. Stingaree Burke was already up and about on business of his own; he was splashing at the washbench behind the kitchen when Compton met him.

"You slept well," the old lawyer told Compton. "Like a man who has nothing on his conscience to disturb his slumbers."

"Perhaps I made excuses for myself," Compton answered with a smile. "What are you grinning about? You look like a cat full of cream."

"You've made me mighty happy, and taken a load off my mind, Charley," Burke said earnestly. "I'm getting on in years, and Mona Belle is my only kin. I don't have to ask; I *know* you will always think of her before yourself."

"Look who's riding in for grub," Burke whispered. "Gospel Cummings and the local law. Morning, men."

"Howdy," Saint John answered. "The top of the morning to you both."

"Likewise," Compton said dryly. "Didn't you sleep well, Gospel?" he asked.

"I slept well, but not long enough," Cummings replied. "I hope you find the treasure of Vallejo today; it has cost enough lives."

"Mostly outlaws," Burke said carelessly. "Call it Destiny, if you will. They coveted their neighbors' goods."

"You lifted that from context," Cummings reproved gravely. "There is another commandment to which men pay little heed."

Shorty Benson and Tom Brady were saddling horses when the search party approached the big solid barn. Stingaree Burke drew Benson aside and whispered to him; the stocky cowboy nodded vigorously. Each rider made sure of his saddle-gear before mounting, a double check which had become a daily habit with all who lived in the saddle.

They left the Circle F yard at a walk just as the

sun came up behind the distant Vermillion Cliffs. While no word had been spoken, Charley Compton rode in the lead with Mona Belle.

"Fine-looking couple, and as fine as they look," Ace Fleming said to Stingaree Burke. "Nature is like that," he continued. "Leave it alone long enough, Nature will take its own course."

"We always realize that fact after it has happened," Burke said earnestly. "I feel ten years younger than I did when I rode up here to tend bar for the late Pug Jones."

"I'd like to know," Fleming said with a frown. "Why did you allow Mona Belle to sing in the Red Rose?"

"That puzzle we were speaking about," the old lawyer explained. "We had a few pieces to the puzzle. We knew that Jones was mixed up with a Syndicate. What we did not know was that he was the head man. We knew Cord Demingway was up here, looking for the treasure."

"Swifty Matthews," Fleming asked. "Where did he fit in?"

"Tim Kelly knew where Matthews was," Burke explained. "He could have arrested Swifty at any time, but he knew that Matthews would not get a fair trial with all those lying witnesses parading against him."

"So you sent him up against Demingway," Fleming guessed.

"Partly," Burke admitted. "And partly to get in

with Pug Jones. We figured that because Swifty was
on the dodge, he would be accepted."

"He wasn't," Fleming said positively. "I knew that
the day I saw him riding with you and Kelly."

"I heard of a plot to kill Swifty," Burke explained.
"Two of the gang got drunk; I was serving them. I
sent word to Swifty to stay out in the brush. You
know the rest from there; we had to bring him in to
the Circle F to keep him from getting dry-gulched."

When Charley and Mona reached the cave at Lost
River, they waited for Ace Fleming to ride up with
Stingaree Burke, closely followed by Saint John and
Gospel Cummings. Cummings glanced at the wheel
tracks which stopped at the foot of the steep trail. He
made no comment, but every one knew that those
tracks had been made by the wagons of the dead.
Boot Hill Crandall had wasted no time.

Cummings took the lead after tying his horse in a
thicket of mesquite bushes. John Saint John followed
the gaunt plainsman with a rifle in his big blocky
hands. Then came Mona Belle and Charley Compton, Fleming and Burke.

They entered the big cave and stood just inside for
a time until their eyes had shed the bright sunlight.
Mona Belle could hear the deep roaring murmur of
the underground river which had given the huge
cave its name. She came closer to Compton, and he
put a protecting arm about her slim waist.

"Yonder is the shelf like an altar," he explained.

"That pile of earth you see came from the pit Cord Demingway started. Up above the shelf is the chimney where the bats come and go, thousands of them."

Ace Fleming watched Saint John with interest. He expected the big deputy sheriff to assert his authority and direct operations. Saint John looked at Charley Compton and spoke in a low, quiet voice.

"It's your party from here on, Charley," he said slowly. "You give the orders, and we will carry them out."

"Now I feel like I was back home on Rancho Vallejo," Compton said with a broad, almost disbelieving smile. "Saint and Gospel will go down in the pit with me to do the first digging. But before we start, we better study this old map some more."

"Study nothing," Ace Fleming declared flatly. "I studied that map so much I know it as well as you do, and you memorized every line, every dot and dash!"

"Right, especially the dots," Compton agreed. "But let's look at it anyway."

He hunkered down on his boot heels and spread the old worn map on the limestone floor. The others gathered about him, watching with interest. Charley Compton cleared his throat.

"We all know the directions to get here," he began. "We know that the map says the hiding place is twenty-two paces north from the mouth of the cave to that shelf yonder. We know it lies between two lime-stone pillars at the base of the shelf."

"And we likewise know it says to dig down ten feet," Fleming said heavily.

"It doesn't say that," Compton contradicted quietly.

"I'll bet you—" Fleming trapped his lips on the unfinished sentence. "I never bet on the other man's game," he corrected himself. "But excuse me if I point. Follow my finger and read it out loud slow."

He leaned over the map, established the due points east and west, and stopped on a single line. *"10 ft. D N."* he read aloud. "You can't make anything else out of it."

"I can," Charley Compton contradicted firmly. "Notice that what you take for *Down* is a capital D and a Capital N. I admit I made one little change. I took my pen knife the night old Jose Morales died. There was a dot, or a period, between the D and the N, and I carefully erased it with the point of my knife. Then I rubbed the place with the burnished part of my knife. That one line once read: '10 ft. *due North!*' Not *down*."

"I'll be damned!" Stingaree Burke ejaculated. "What are we waiting for?" he shouted.

"For strong backs and willing hearts," Compton said with a smile, and he was the first one down in the hole. He took the lantern Fleming handed down, and lighted the way for Cummings and John Saint John.

"I wondered why you brought that pick-bar," Cummings said with sudden understanding.

Compton took the short iron bar, attacked some rotting timbers which had appeared to be shoring to hold back the dirt, and easily pried them loose. Then he stepped back to make room for the two big men.

"Ten feet due north," he said quietly. Gospel Cummings and Saint John began to swing their picks. "This didn't need any shoring," the deputy remarked, after a few minutes of toil. "That shelf above us is solid limestone, and it makes a perfect arch."

After an hour, they were under the arch. Ace Fleming and Charley Compton climbed into the hole and began to shovel out the dirt the two big men tossed into the hole from under the rocky shelf. After two hours of furious digging, Ace Fleming suggested a short rest.

"After all," he said wearily, "if that old treasure laid there a hundred years, a couple of hours won't make any difference."

"So I'll spell you," Compton suggested. "We ought to be close."

As Fleming climbed out of the deep hole, Mona Belle climbed down to join Compton.

"Are you sure it will make no difference, Charley," she asked anxiously, "if we do find the old treasure?"

"Positive," he said, as he kissed her.

Then he released himself and took the pick-bar. He worked for a few moments, turned his head to listen when the bar struck a rotting timber, and seized the pick. Ten minutes later he went to his knees and made a few quick strokes with the pick. Then he called softly to Mona Belle who joined him under the shelf.

"Look," he said. "The Vallejo treasure!"

Mona Belle reached out a hand and touched a bar of dull metal. "The gold bullion," she whispered.

"There must be a ton of it," Compton said huskily. "Let's call Stingaree!"

The lawyer climbed down into the hole like an eager youngster, followed by Fleming and Cummings. They stared at the dull bars of stained metal, piled neatly like cord-wood, with bits of rotting wood and leather here and there.

"They packed this gold up here on mules," Cummings said slowly. "Funny how much difference a dot can make here and there. Now I know why Charley was not worried when he saw that Demingway had started to dig."

Mona Belle reached well back and picked up a sodden square object. It was a lead box about a foot square, soldered all along the top edges. Stingaree Burke produced a knife and carefully worked on the heavy lid. When at last he lifted the stained metal, a shower of flashes winked back at them from the interior.

"Oh!" Mona Belle gasped. "Diamonds and rubies and emeralds. Hundreds of them!"

"A hundred years ago that was the easiest way to convert money into wealth," Burke explained quietly. "My dear, allow me to congratulate you. You have found the treasure of Rancho Vallejo!"

Charley Compton was on his knees, reaching into the depths of the hole under the rocky shelf. His face was grimy with dirt, and his shirt was soiled and torn. He stopped for a moment, took a deep breath, and then brought out a smaller lead box, pitted with age.

"I hope I am right," he said quietly. "This should be worth more than all the gold and jewels." He handed the box to Burke, who cut away the natural lead solder which sealed the receptacle.

There was a deep silence while the old lawyer worked on the leaden box. Only the heavy breathing of the six workers could be heard above the murmuring roar of Lost River. Charley Compton watched intently; he grasped Mona Belle's right hand tightly.

Stingaree Burke carefully placed the blade of his knife under the heavy lead lid. He pried gently, exerted more pressure, and the lid raised slowly. Burke stared at a bit of stained oiled silk in the box. He lifted it gently, passed the box to Saint John, and leaned closer to the lantern. A silken cord broke under his fingers, and the old lawyer carefully unwrapped a folded parchment.

He exposed an ancient document heavy with brilliant red and gold seals, written entirely in Spanish. He turned to Mona Belle with a smile.

"*Señorita,* please to translate for us," he said politely.

Mona Belle leaned over, still holding tightly to Compton's hand. "It is the land grant, measured in leagues," she whispered. "To Don Alvarado Vallejo, his heirs and their heirs forever. In the year of our Lord 1802. Thank you, Charley," she said earnestly. "Now our people will never have to leave Rancho Vallejo!"

"Just a minute," Saint John interrupted. "Here's a note on an old piece of paper in the bottom of this lead box. I can't make head nor tail out of it."

"Let me see it," Mona Belle asked quickly.

"It's from Don Alvarado," she said breathlessly, after glancing at the aged note. "Listen to this!" she cried. "It is almost as though Don Alvarado were writing to Charley."

> "*Thieves will try to rob me, and find the treasure. I have the feeling that an honest man will at last be successful in the cave of Lost River. To him, I bequeath and bestow half the amount of the gold and jewels on one condition: that he use it wisely to restore Rancho Vallejo. Signed: Alvarado Vallejo.*"

There was a silence for a moment, and then the deep resonant voice of Stingaree Burke spoke softly. "Mona Belle, you will marry a wealthy man!"

"And an honest one," Ace Fleming added heartily. "Let's climb up out of this pit!"

Stingaree Burke folded the land grant, wrapped it again in the oiled silk, and replaced it in the small casket. "I will file this document with the land commissioner," he declared with satisfaction. "I am just thankful that the Syndicate did not find it first!"

He climbed out of the hole, followed by Saint John who carried the heavy box of jewels. Charley Compton helped Mona Belle, and he was like a man just awakening from a deep sleep. He was a legal part-owner of the vast Rancho Vallejo which had always carried the Box V brand.

"Stand and deliver!" a rough voice said loudly. "I'll shoot the first man who makes a move for his gun!"

"Dude Fargo!" Stingaree Burke said hoarsely.

"The same, and now head of the Syndicate," Fargo said thickly. "I was hiding all the time on that shelf, letting you shovel hands do the hard work for me. Just lay that land grant there on the floor. Put the jewels along with it, and step back. I've got two guns on you, and mine are clean!"

Charley Compton listened with his head turned partly to the side. He glanced down at his dirty clothing; stared at the six-shooter riding deep, and jammed in holster leather.

"I'm watching you, Fleming," Fargo said viciously. "Just do what you were thinking about!"

"You can't get us both," Fleming said boldly. "I'm a gambler, Fargo. If you shoot me, Charley Compton will get you before you can ear back for a follow-up!"

Charley Compton straightened suddenly. Ace Fleming was giving him a message, and Fleming was a gambler. Fleming spoke again.

"I always play the cards fate deals me," he told Fargo. "Every smart hombre does the same. You're dealing this hand, and you coppered your bet like a cheap tin-horn!"

"So get brave and make a pass for your irons," Fargo sneered. "I've got *two* guns, remember? I don't have to ear back for a follow-up!"

"Do as he says, Ace," Saint John said hoarsely, and he placed the lead cask of jewels on the ground.

"Yes, please," Mona Belle added her importunities.

Stingaree Burke leaned over and placed the land grant near the casket of jewels. Without warning, Ace Fleming threw himself to the ground and to the right. A gun blasted viciously, and orange flame spurted from the right hand of Dude Fargo.

Charley Compton knew it was coming; he had been trained to read sign from boyhood. His right hand darted down and up with scarcely a pause to separate the two movements. His gun roared thunderously just as Fargo was swinging around to trigger the weapon in his left hand.

Dude Fargo gasped and dropped his smoking guns in the deep pit. He followed them in a headlong dive as his knees buckled. Ace Fleming rolled up from behind a thick limestone pillar, and he limped slightly as he came into the light from the lantern.

"Close," he said with a shrug. "He shot the heel from my left boot!"

Saint John sighed and lowered himself to the pit. He took the lantern Fleming handed down, made a brief examination, and climbed back out.

"The deceased is dead," he said simply. "Through the heart."

"Horses outside," Burke said quickly. "Looks like a string of pack horses to me."

"That will be Tom Brady and Shorty Benson," Fleming said casually. "I figured Charley knew where that treasure was, and I played the hunch. Six pack horses; that ought to be enough to move the gold ingots."

## CHAPTER FIFTEEN

Stingaree Burke stood in the Circle F yard, staring at the stacked ingots of gold. The old lawyer had changed to a black broadcloth suit, white shirt, walking boots, and neat black Stetson. Gospel Cummings could have passed for the lawyer's twin, if Burke had been ten years younger. Cummings' long-tailed coat was green with age, but both men were tall and angular, and seasoned with age.

"Phoenix is the nearest point where it would be safe to ship the bullion on the railroad," Cummings suggested. "I know a preacher in Phoenix."

The two men appraised each other, and Burke smiled. "The sooner the quicker," he agreed.

"We will have to make up quite a sizable escort to guard the gold on the pack-trip," Burke continued. "Both Mona Belle and Charley will want to go, and we can spring the wedding on them as a surprise when we reach Phoenix."

"Agreed," Cummings answered just above a whisper. "Quiet now; yonder they come together."

Charley Compton approached the pair with Mona Belle, holding the girl's left hand. Mona Belle was radiant with happiness, and Compton seemed like a different man.

"Mona Belle and I wanted to talk to you old mossy-horns," Compton began confidently. "The gold will have to be packed out to Phoenix, and we are both going along, of course. So we decided that it would be nice for us to get married in Phoenix."

Stingaree Burke and Gospel Cummings stared at each other. Cummings sought refuge from his embarrassment by stroking his long brown beard. Stingaree Burke felt for the makings, spilled tobacco into a brown paper, and slowly rolled a smoke.

"Good idea," he said heartily. "Capital!"

"Likewise," Cummings agreed. "I know a preacher down in Phoenix who will tie the knot so tight it amounts to a life sentence."

"That's for me," Compton said earnestly, "Mona Belle and I will trot in double harness for the rest of our lives. Gospel, will you be my best man?"

"Glad to," Cummings answered with a happy smile. "And who will be bridesmaid?"

"Sandra Fleming," Mona Belle answered. "Little Deloise will be flower-girl. Charley and I want to thank you both for all you have done for us."

Cummings excused himself and walked into the big barn. His hands were trembling as he reached into the right tail of his coat. He brought out the familiar quart of Three Daisies, made a mark with his thumb, and drank down past the mark. After another one for the road, he replaced the bottle, and the tremble had left his strong brown hands. He was leaving the barn when a shadow darkened the doorway.

Cummings glanced up and stared at Swifty Matthews, who carried a pair of saddle-bags across his left arm. His right was in a bandanna sling, but Matthews was dressed for the trails. He smiled when he saw Cummings, reached down inside the sling which supported his arm, and handed Cummings a stiff paper.

"Will you throw my hull on my horse, Gospel?" he asked. "And give the paper to Mona Belle for a wedding present. It's the deed to that land I won in a poker game from Joe Demingway down in Laredo."

"Glad to do it, Swifty," Cummings answered gently, and he did not embarrass the tall Texan with questions. He knew that Matthews wanted to leave at once; he too had once loved a beautiful girl, and had lost.

"Good luck, Swifty," he said quietly.

Cummings watched him ride away into the setting sun. It reminded him of another lonely ride when, because of his one besetting sin, he had left Sandra's mother to a better man. . . .

Ace Fleming knew the Wells Fargo agent in Phoenix, and after the gold was safely delivered, he took Mona Belle and Sandra to a comfortable hotel. The men put up at another small hotel, and Gospel Cummings went to see his friend about the wedding. Stingaree Burke had wired a wealthy gem dealer in San Francisco to meet him in Phoenix, and the two were closeted in a locked room for several hours.

The wedding was set for the following afternoon, and Compton wandered around like a lost soul. Sandra and Mona Belle were making the most of every minute, and as Skid Yancey remarked: "putting it on mean."

"I'm glad I only have to get married once," Compton said irritably. "This sorter thing almost kills a

man, and the women enjoy every minute of the
agony."

Charley Compton fidgeted in a big chair until Gospel Cummings came from his room and announced
that it was time to ride to the Preacher's. They could
have hired a surrey, but Shorty Benson insisted that a
horse was a cowboy's best friend, and had the horses
waiting at the tie-rail in front of the little hotel.

Charley Compton's knees were knocking together
as he followed Gospel Cummings into the parlor of
the parsonage. Ace Fleming waited with the preacher,
who shook hands with Cummings and Compton. He
motioned with his head to a staircase leading to the
second floor.

"The ladies will be down at once," he said in an
echoing whisper.

His wife was seated at a little pump organ. She
smiled at Charley Compton, poised her hands above
the keys, and began to pump the organ. Then she
began to play the strains of the wedding march.

Gospel Cummings stood up and helped Compton
to his feet. All eyes were turned to the staircase, and
Mona Belle came into view on the arm of Stingaree
Burke. Mona Belle carried a bridal bouquet of red
roses and lilies of the valley. She wore a white satin
gown with a long trail. Sandra Fleming followed
with a bouquet of roses, and little Deloise darted here
and there strewing flowers on the white linen which
covered the stairs.

Mona Belle was smiling with happiness, and thoroughly relaxed. Stingaree Burke looked past the preacher and winked at Charley Compton. Charley swallowed noisily and tried to find something to do with his hands. They felt twice as big as usual, and he shifted on his new polished boots.

"Who giveth this woman in marriage?" the preacher asked quietly.

"I do," Stingaree Burke answered proudly, and he placed Mona Belle's left hand in Charley Compton's right.

"Charley ain't a-going to make it," Yancey whispered to Benson, "unless Mona Belle holds him up!"

Mona Belle tightened her grip on Compton's hand. The ceremony began, and Compton listened like a man in a trance. The preacher's voice seemed to come from a great distance, but at last the ordeal was over. Gospel Cummings handed Compton the wedding ring, and when the preacher had pronounced them man and wife, Mona Belle slid into Compton's arms.

"Kiss me," she prompted softly. "Charley!"

Charley Compton obeyed mechanically. Then he seemed to awaken as his lips met those of this lovely bride. His arms tightened about her, and his face changed as the healthy color returned.

"I'll try my best to make you happy, Missus Compton," he whispered in Mona Belle's ear. "You looked like a dream."

"And you acted like you were having one," Mona

Belle said with a little laugh.

"Congratulations, Charley," Stingaree Burke interrupted. "Line up behind me to kiss the bride!"

At last they were outside, and Burke led Charley Compton to the surrey. "You ride with your wife," he said sternly. "I'll ride your horse back to the hotel. Did you buy your train tickets yet?"

"Gosh no," Compton stammered.

"Was you figuring to ride back to Laredo horseback?" the old lawyer asked sharply.

"Come to think about it, I just didn't think about it," Compton confessed manfully. "I was in a sorter fog, but my head has cleared some now."

"So I bought the tickets for you," Burke said with a smile. "You leave on the morning train, and I leave at midnight."

The train trip seemed all too short for the bride and groom. Stingaree Burke was waiting with horses when they arrived at Laredo, and the old lawyer seemed to have shed a decade of years. He explained what he had done as they rode out to the Rancho Vallejo for a homecoming which he assured the happy couple would be their last.

"The commissioner will issue a deed with the boundaries as marked by the old land grant," he told them. "The jewel dealer in San Francisco will give four hundred thousand dollars for the gems, but I kept these out for the bride."

He stopped his Box V horse and handed a velvet

case to Mona Belle. The bright Texas sunlight reflected back from a collection of unset diamonds, rubies and emeralds, and Mona Belle gasped and feasted on their beauty.

"Thank you, Uncle," she said in a low voice. "We will keep them always. They belong to Charley and me, just like everything else on the Rancho Vallejo!"

After Burke had gone, Charley Compton turned to Mona Belle and took her in his arms. "Home again, darling," he said tenderly. "We will build up the ranch the way Don Alvarado intended. I wonder what old Gospel Cummings would say?"

Mona Belle smiled and kissed her husband. "Gospel is one of the finest men I have ever known," she said loyally. "Let's send him a fine new Bible; that old one is about worn out."

"And a case of Three Daisies," Compton added. "Gospel is a man with a dual personality, and we don't want him to get lopsided!"